TRUE STORIES

DAVID BYRNE

WITH PHOTOGRAPHS BY

WILLIAM EGGLESTON, LEN JENSHEL, MARK LIPSON, AND DAVID BYRNE

PENGUIN BOOKS

PENGUIN BOOKS
Viking Penguin Inc., 40 West 23rd Street,
New York, New York 10010, U.S.A.
Penguin Books Ltd, Harmondsworth,
Middlesex, England
Penguin Books Australia Ltd, Ringwood,
Victoria, Australia
Penguin Books Canada Limited, 2801 John Street,
Markham, Ontario, Canada L3R 1B4
Penguin Books (N.Z.) Ltd, 182-190 Wairau Road,
Auckland 10, New Zealand

First published in Penguin Books 1986
Published simultaneously in Canada

Library of Congress Cataloging-in-Publication Data

Byrne, David, 1952–
   True stories.

   I. Title.
PN1997.T7155   1986   791.43'72   86-2537
ISBN 0-14-009230-7

Produced by Roundtable Press, Inc.
Design: Katy Homans and David Byrne
Design Assistant: Bethany Johns
Editorial Assistants: Marguerite Ross, Betty Vera
Composition: Trufont Typographers
Book Production: Paul Levin, Giga Communications, Inc.
Color Separations: Reprocolor Llovet
Printing and Binding: W. A. Krueger Company
Front Cover Photograph: Mark Lipson
Cover Design: Katy Homans and David Byrne

Printed in the United States of America

Set in Sabon and Univers

BOOK CREDITS

Coordinator	Holland Sutton
Designer	Katy Homans and David Byrne
Editor	Nan Graham
Production	Marsha Melnick
Special thanks to:	Karen Murphy
	Adelle Lutz
	Tibor Kalman
	Bridget DeSocio

DB

CHARACTERS

NARRATOR

LOUIS FYNE

LAZY WOMAN

MR. TUCKER

EARL CULVER

KAY CULVER

CUTE WOMAN

RAMON

LYING WOMAN

CAST

Louis Fyne	John Goodman
Kay Culver	Anne McEnroe
Earl Culver	Spalding Gray
Narrator	David Byrne
Lazy Woman	Swoosie Kurtz
Lying Woman	Jo Harvey Allen
Mr. Tucker	Roebuck "Pops" Staples
Cute Woman	Alix Elias
Ramon	Tito Larriva
Computer Guy	Matthew Posey
Preacher	John Ingle

FILM CREDITS

Director	David Byrne
Screenplay	David Byrne,
	Beth Henley, Stephen Tobolowsky
Executive Producer	Ed Pressman
Producer	Gary Kurfirst
Co-Producer	Karen Murphy
Director of Photography	Ed Lachman
Film Editor	Caroline Biggerstaff
Production Designer	Barbara Ling
Casting Director	Victoria Thomas
Sound Designer	Leslie Shatz
Songs Recorded by	Talking Heads
Special thanks to:	Mo Austin
	Jeff Ayeroff
	Steve Baker
	Meredith Monk
	Christina Patoski
	Adelle Lutz
	Joan Tewkesbury
	Jonathan Demme
	Texas Film Commission

INTRODUCTION

DAVID BYRNE

WITH PHOTOGRAPHS BY WILLIAM EGGLESTON

This film began, not as one story or script, but with a lot of stories found in various newspaper articles, along with some dramatic visual ideas represented by drawings I made. Movies are a combination of sounds and pictures, and stories are a trick to get you to keep paying attention. With a few exceptions, almost all the story ideas in the movie came out of tabloid newspapers, most notably the *Weekly World News*. I couldn't have made this stuff up. I just found the pieces and put them together. I began collecting articles while Talking Heads were on tour in 1983, the *Stop Making Sense* tour. All the articles that ended up being adapted for the film are in this book. Some of the visual ideas represented by the drawings didn't make it into the film. Some of these remain in the book as storyboards. The script and drawings became the framework for the film.

The way this film framework was constructed was inspired a little bit by my work with Robert Wilson, by his working process. He often begins work on a theater piece with mainly visual ideas and then layers the sound and dialogue on top of that. I used a similar method. I covered a wall with drawings, most of them representing events that could take place in one town. Then I reordered the drawings, again and again, until they seemed to have some sort of flow. Meanwhile I assigned the characters inspired by the tabloid newspaper articles to the people represented in the drawings.

I then tried to integrate the music in the film into the time and the region. I hope the songs have some of the flavor and texture of the regional music found in Texas. The songs occur through-out the film in more or less their natural setting. People don't suddenly burst into song for unjustified reasons, as they did in old-fashioned musicals. Neither do they pantomime a story, as they do in rock videos. Instead, the songs expand on the personalities of the characters and on the milieu in and around the town where the story is set. Although the songs don't necessarily advance the story line, they do give relatively placid people—like you or me—a justification for becoming vibrant and full of energy, for expressing themselves and exposing their insides to everyone else in the town. In many cases, the depth of feeling and strength of the people is revealed through the songs and not through their daily activities.

I had ordered a series of dramatic events and songs, represented by the drawings on the wall, but there was still no story, no trick to pull you through, to keep your attention, and to tie one thing to another. So I worked with a couple of writers, Beth Henley and Steven Tobolowsky. Together we found the story, and they wrote the first draft of a script. We went a little too far. The script had too much story in it. It didn't allow for enough tangential activity in the film. So I revised the script about three times. The story line changed; it became more fragmented; and other devices were substituted to keep things rolling along.

In *True Stories* I stay away from loaded subjects—sex, violence, and political intrigue—because as soon as you get on those subjects, everybody already has preconceived ideas about them. I deal with stuff that's too dumb for people to have bothered to formulate opinions on.

During this period of revisions, I knew I would eventually have to explain to other people what I wanted the film to look like. It's a pretty impossible thing to do in words, so to explain it, and as a way of getting random inspiration, I began to look, over and over again, at books of photography and the work of various photographers. Two recent books—surveys of new color photography—were really useful. With these I could show somebody a photograph by William Eggleston or Len Jenshel or Joel Sternfeld or Stuart Klipper, among others, and say, "This is the kind of color I want in this scene, and this is the way I envision this room" or "This is the kind of look I'm thinking about for this character." It was really exciting, and it was a lot of fun. The only problem was that everywhere I went, I had to lug a suitcase full of books around.

Ed Lachman, the director of photography, and I would pore over these books discussing how each scene would look; and Barbara Ling, the production designer, and I would look at them and talk about the way the houses should look, and inside the houses and inside the churches, and what it was like where people worked and where they went to school and where they walked and where they shopped. It seems kind of fitting that in a way this project started with books of pictures and here we are with a book of pictures again. And some of the same photographers are represented.

I'm hoping that this book will be the equivalent of the way we experience people and things in their environments. Out there lots of different things are going on at the same time. You can change your focus from one thing to another and still keep the first thing in your mind. You can look through other people's eyes, or look with a changing point of view, at the same place. You can stand at one spot and focus on different things and really look at them in different ways simultaneously. It's an effect that sometimes can be achieved in the theater, but it's almost impossible to do in film. It's easier in a book.

In this book we've tried to arrange the pages so that, moving from left to right on each page, you get progressively further away from the actual film. Beginning with the script on the far left and then moving to the right are, first, the storyboards and stills from the actual film. Further over are the research materials that inspired parts of the story, and then even further over are images which are not in the film and sometimes don't even pretend to illustrate what's on the left-hand side of the page. But they have some other kind of connection.

Originally *True Stories* wasn't set in Texas. I didn't know where it was going to be, but at some point someone suggested that I look at Texas. After the first trip it was hard to think of the story as taking place anywhere else. The people in Texas and the people who gravitate there have always had this fiercely independent spirit. While they may not be tolerant of a lot of things, they seem to be fairly tolerant of personal eccentricities. There's enough room in Texas for people to live their personal lives any way they want. Whatever works for you is OK. This leads to a lot of excess. Texas also has good film crews, facilities, a wide variety of different kinds of indigenous music: gospel, cumbia, country and western, rock, polkas, and blues, to name a few.

Most of all, Texas looked great. It didn't look that different from anywhere else, there was just more of it. It was the same but more. The flat landscapes were great. Besides affecting people's attitudes and ways of living, they make everything look cool. For film it's really graphic. Anything you stick in there is just about all there is to look at. You can't look at a picture of it and go, "Well, is this image about the tree or the house or the person driving up in the car or the building in the background or the street or the tunnel or the flagpole or that hill back there or the house that's on the hill or the flowing stream?" It doesn't even occur to you to ask, because in this landscape there's only one thing happening in front of you; all the extraneous items are gone. I suppose it's an existential landscape . . . . Stick some people out there, they're all on their own. Things look like they just suddenly have been plopped down there. And there's a tremendous amount of construction.

American towns expand in concentric rings. At the moment the center of most urban doughnuts is a hole. The modern urban center maybe has some new glass office buildings in it but it's just a shell for people to work in. There's no life there. Nobody really lives there. In smaller towns, like Virgil, at least the original Main Street is left. Around the urban center is a ring of lower buildings, beautiful old dwellings that are now in disrepair. These are the buildings that were abandoned when white people fled to the suburbs. Now these same people and their sons and daughters are beginning to move back in and restore these buildings. The condition of these buildings has gone from being grand, to a state of disrepair and decay, to a state of . . . cute.

Beyond this ring of urban decay and now gentrification, there's usually a highway or ring road or some kind of freeway that circles the whole town. Along these freeways are bumps of clean industry interspersed with newer residential areas. Beginning at this ring and expanding outward are loads of houses being built out onto the plains. Many people who were raised in falling-down old houses, well, now they want something new. They don't want to get married and live in another falling-down old house, so they move out here. The construction may not be as sturdy, but it's brand new. It's theirs. (I have something to say about the difference between American cities and European cities but I forget what it is. I've got it written down at home somewhere.) Americans have totally ignored or forgotten what, for Europeans, are the unwritten laws that govern what makes a city liveable. They're proving that you can make a city work even if people can't tell it's working.

Trammell Crow, Sr., was just finishing up the Info Mart while we were shooting *True Stories*. It's one of the weirdest pieces of architecture ever, a huge trade mart devoted to the microelectronics industry, modeled after the Crystal Palace or maybe it was the Brighton Pavilion. It's like trying to make a computer look like a grandfather clock.

If you can think of it, if you can imagine it, it exists somewhere. The largest shopping center in the world has a really long serpentine lake in the middle of it, and five submarines go up and down it. The waters are infested with sharks and surrounded by jungle. I couldn't have made this up. It's in Edmonton, Canada. It exists. True story: I was just recently told about a man in Texas who's soliciting funds to build a wall around the state modeled after the Great Wall of China.

It takes people here to have the audacity to build something like the Info Mart and make it work. You feel like you're laughing at it and admiring it at the same time. It's a great feeling. Kind of cheers you up. In my various research trips to Texas I looked around and I could see where the dramatic events in *True Stories* could take place and who would be there and what it would look like. I could redraw all the storyboards based on real people. It became clear where the different characters' lives would overlap and where they would run into each other. The story is just a trick to hold your attention. It opens the door and lets the real movie in.

Movie making is a trick. Song writing is a trick. If a song is done really well, the trick works. If not, people can see through it right away. Maybe this movie can be a trick and show you how the trick is done at the same time. Maybe this book can kind of do that too. Most movies show you something and tell you how you're supposed to feel about it. They're edited in a way that tells you what you're supposed to be looking at before you decide that's what you want to be looking at. It's a trick, and when it doesn't work, it's really offensive, because you know someone's trying to trick you, and they think you can't tell.

The new patriotism is also a trick. It's a real frightening, scary trick that everyone wants so badly to believe is true. The government is selling the country down the river. The real wealth of the country is in the people.

Empires in retreat get into some pretty weird stuff. Egypt, Rome, England, Japan, Spain, and now the United States. They get this intense pride and nostalgia for what they imagine they are and what they imagine they were because they can see it

slipping away. America had a lot of free money for a long time. Money that came out of the ground. In Texas it just shot right out of the ground. All you had to do was look around and find it. When cheap slave labor ran out we just brought some over from overseas. The expansion got a little out of hand, but it's over now. Some of us might have seen the tail end of the heyday, but now most of us can feel reality settling in.

Some people think it's the end of the world; they think Jesus is going to come. He didn't come when Nero fiddled. Why should he come for us? Some people think outsiders are dragging us down. Some people think we just got on the wrong diets—not eating enough vegetables. Some people think we can jog away the fat. Some people get depressed and turn to drugs or drinking. Some people get depressed and go to parties—getting all dressed up for the end of the world. Some people are going to escape into a space station to live on artificial worlds. Some people turn inside themselves or go to India. Some people are investing in real estate. Some people go to school and try to analyze the situation. Some people are arming themselves, storing up ammunition and cans of food, getting ready for the invasion. Some people are waiting for the visitors from outer space to come, getting ready for the landing, and preparing a welcome.

Tab with vitamins. Diet cola with vitamins . . . . That's a sure sign. Some of these people are here, in this movie. Some of them we left out.

Then there's the other kind of people. People who seem to have found some kind of ethical center. They might be floundering around a little bit but it's a noble kind of floundering. Sometimes it's hard to tell one kind from the other.

For years we have been taught not to like things. Finally somebody said it was OK to like things. This was a great relief. It was getting hard to go around not liking everything. The thing about it is, all of these people are right. None of them is wrong. They are setting a good example, and in this film and book I'm teaching myself to appreciate them. Besides, it was a lot of fun.

About the photographs in this book.

Most of the photographs in this book are by William Eggleston, Len Jenshel, Mark Lipson, and me. The ones in this introduction are by William Eggleston. He was using a Leica and buying his film from the drugstore. The more of Eggleston's pictures you look at together, the more you can feel his sensibility and his way of looking taking you over like kudzu or some kind of insidious creeping moss. Individual pictures are sometimes hard to figure out. Sometimes you think there's kind of nothing there, but when you see a lot of Eggleston's pictures at once you can feel what it must be like behind his eyeballs. His current project, the Democratic Forest, consists of 15,000 pictures. He's probably the only one who's seen them all.

Len Jenshel came in from New York and we thought he shouldn't concentrate too much on what we were doing at the set each day. He brought a handmade 6×9cm camera that looked like a slightly overgrown 35mm but got a pretty good sized negative. We agreed that he would go out and get representative landscapes and buildings and people that in a way showed we weren't filming in a vacuum. Characters and situations just like the ones we were filming existed all around us.

Mark Lipson drove in from L.A. and stayed around the set for most of our shooting days. He took pictures from the movie camera's point of view or of the production process.

My photos were taken mostly while on location-scouting trips. Actually the trips were kind of excuses for taking pictures. Occasionally, I'd take pictures from the movie-camera point of view when no one else with a camera was around.

Fade in: Exterior Flat Texas Landscape—(Day)

A road extends directly away from the CAMERA into the distance. The landscape is completely flat ... like a line drawn across the middle of the FRAME. No trees, no houses or other interruptions. We hear the SOUNDS of INSECTS and BIRDS.

We can just make out a figure in the distance ... walking toward us ... As it comes closer, we see it is a LITTLE GIRL. She is dressed plainly, but not poorly. She is about 8 to 10 years old. She has an innocent but all-knowing look about her.

As she gets closer, we become aware of a new series of SOUNDS ... emerging out of the "natural" ones. It becomes apparent that these sounds are being produced by the GIRL. They are uncanny vocal imitations of natural sounds.

Her figure now fills the frame ... She begins executing a series of wondrous and strange gestures, in a rather contemplative manner ... and as if for her own amusement.

Her gestures are somewhat repetitive, but not stiff ... They are relaxed and comfortable, but well thought out ... as if they were another language.

The SOUNDS of MUSICAL INSTRUMENTS are heard faintly now, as her face fills the screen.

Joining these sounds is the VOICE of the NARRATOR, which is friendly and straightforward.

NARRATOR (VOICE-OVER) This is where the town begins. This part of the country has been through lots of changes ... and not all small ones either. I think they're in the process of going through another one.

The SOUNDS of the MUSIC begin to replace those of the LITTLE GIRL.

NARRATOR (V.O.) There is bound to be at least one person who remembers when everything here was just open land ... like right here ... Some people can look at the land ... just *look* at it ... and tell you what happened there.

DB

Still Photo of an Ocean ... Very Similar to the Landscape

The LITTLE GIRL'*s sounds have stopped.*

NARRATOR (V.O.)   This whole area was once under-water ... Kind of looks like it, doesn't it?

Title: "True Stories"

NARRATOR (V.O.)   After that there was a period when the dinosaurs roamed over the landscape ... I used to be fascinated by dinosaurs when I was a kid ...

Pan Panoramic Drawing of Dinosaurs

... a lot of guys were. Chthyosaurus swam in the seas of Central Texas ... They looked a lot like porpoises.

Photo of Glen Rose Dinosaur Facsimile

Jaws wide enough to gobble a golf cart. Recently ...

Photo of "Lady Bird" Johnson or Other Well-known Texas Woman

NARRATOR (V.O.)   ... the bones of a woman from 20,000 years ago were found. "Midland Minnie" she was nicknamed.

Photo (Black and White) of a Few Scattered People on the Flat Landscape

NARRATOR (V.O.)   Early inhabitants referred to themselves as "the people."

Photo of backyard barb-b-que

NARRATOR (V.O.)   Other groups were referred to as "friends." The word "Texas" comes from the Cad-doan word for friend.

Dinosaurs

Dinosaurs never really seemed real. They were like a fairy tale that was supported and justified by science ... as phony as any fairy tale. The disappearance of the dinosaurs, of course, is still a great mystery. My favorite theory is that they were wiped out when a different kind of foliage began to predominate and they all became constipated.

It's curious that dinosaurs are used as metaphors for large corporations or outmoded organizations, implying that the body has gotten big and the brain has stayed the same or has evolved to be smaller and smaller. It's also curious that kids like dinosaurs and are fascinated by them but are not as fascinated by living animals that are just as big in size, like elephants or whales. Maybe elephants and whales seem too passive.

Evolution is such a complicated, convoluted explanation, in that more and more explanations are added as more questions are raised. Some kind of revision is probably due because a lot of unexplained connections between things are just being swept under the carpet. Ever since scientific thinking replaced religion and mythology as the dominant explanation for things, scientists have been placed in the role of priests, as the ones who tell people the true explanations of things, but they're involved in just as much petty squabbling and as many ego battles as the priests ever were. Same deal. New outfits.

LJ

Photo of Sammy Davis Jr. hugging Nixon

Another Archival Photo of the Caddo Tribe or Early Pioneers or Little House on the Prairie TV show

NARRATOR (V.O.)   The Caddo were among the first to be wiped out by the early white settlers.

Film or Stock Photo of Violent Storm

NARRATOR (V.O.)   The first Spanish to arrive here were shipwrecked by a hurricane.

Photo of a Side of Beef ... Hunters ... People Eating ... a Period Spanish Man Kissing a Woman on the Neck

NARRATOR (V.O.)   They turned cannibal to survive ... to the horror of the local Indians.

Present-Day News Photos

NARRATOR (V.O.)   It was a pretty hairy time ... One group of Spanish settlers offered the Indians the chance to become slaves ...

Archival Photo ... (Spaniard and Native American Shaking Hands?)

NARRATOR (V.O.)   The Indians thought about it ... decided it was not a good idea, and killed the Spaniards ...

Brief Montage of Old Cowboy-and-Indian and War-Film Battle Scenes Through the Next 5 Statements ... (Boxing Film?)

NARRATOR (V.O.)
The Spaniards fought the Mexicans.
The Mexicans fought the "Americans."
The "Americans" fought the Wichitas.
The Wichitas fought the Tankowas.
The Tankowas fought the Comanches.
And the Comanches fought everyone.

Photo or Film Clip of Spanish-American Musicians . . . Mexican-Americans Living a Good Life . . . Laughing . . . Singing . . . Eating

NARRATOR (V.O.)   Meanwhile, mostly Spanish-speaking people are trying to live here.

Photo of C.I.A. Director . . . C.I.A. Emblem . . . or Group of American "Advisors"

NARRATOR (V.O.)   Covert military operations to seize Texas for the U.S. were begun in 1835.

Photo of Elton John or George Clinton or Similar Celebrity in Wild Frontier Outfit

NARRATOR (V.O.)   One of the leaders of this operation was Sam Houston . . . who often wore a leopard-skin vest . . . a lion-skin cloak . . . a Mexican sombrero . . . and Cherokee blankets and jewelry.

Photo of the Alamo?

NARRATOR (V.O.)   Well, eventually they did get Texas. Land grabbers and railroad companies moved in.

Photos of People Living It Up, Extravagant Wealth, Having Fun, Dressed Up and Having a Good Time

NARRATOR (V.O.)   The economy boomed . . . People got rich.

Camera Panning a Panoramic Photo of the Texas Landscape Filled with Oil Wells

NARRATOR (V.O.)   First on cotton . . . then cattle . . . then oil . . . and *now* . . .

Image of a Hand Holding a Tiny, Tiny Computer Chip

South Central States

Thousands of eager settler-speculators lined up under the gaze of the U.S. cavalry, impatiently awaiting the signal to plunge into the hitherto sacrosanct Indian lands where they had a right under the Homestead Act to claim a 160-acre plot. With the firing of the signal guns at noon on April 22, 1889, people hurled themselves pell-mell on horseback, in wagons or astride mules into the raw, empty land, dismounting with stake hammers to drive hurried claims . . .

Lashed securely to the flooring of many wagons were the parts of a printing press or a barber chair or the office equipment needed to establish an instant bank or real-estate office . . .

Whole towns were raised in a matter of hours; committees were formed, city charters executed and elections held in a matter of days. By evening of the opening day of the rush, several tented cities of 10,000 or more joyful, dust-covered souls had sprouted on the plains . . .

The choicest lots and homesites did not by any means all go to those quickest off the mark when the signal guns sounded. The evidence is conclusive that, as one observer put it, "a considerable part of the population had appeared on the site [of Oklahoma City] within 15 minutes after the noon signal for the run was given—30 miles away!" These early arrivals . . . had slipped over the starting line the night before . . .

Burke Burnett Field, Texas

NARRATOR (V.O.) ...microelectronics.

The silicon-based transistor was first proposed near here in 1949.

Photo of Jack Kilby with a Chip

NARRATOR (V.O.) In 1958, Jack Kilby invented the integrated circuit while he was working at Texas Instruments ...

... He doesn't work there anymore. *Look!* ...

Various Photos of Metal Buildings on the Flat Landscape

NARRATOR (V.O.) Texas is the largest producer of metal buildings. They are not taken all that seriously as buildings ... by a lot of people, but they're the least expensive and the most popular form of industrial construction.

Photos of Similarly Shaped Buildings, but with Stucco, Stone Slab or Wood Facades ... Details of the Coverings

NARRATOR (V.O.) Sometimes they try to disguise them ... but it doesn't really matter ... You grow to like them.

Shots of Objects in the Shape of Texas ... the Camera Begins to Pull Back as the Images Continue to Dissolve One into the Other

NARRATOR (V.O.) This is the 150th anniversary of the State of Texas. Every city is doing something special.

Exterior, Virgil—(Dawn)

Slide Shots of Virgil Main Streets in the Early Morning. Camera Continues to Pull Back

We see some banners across the street ... a few decorations in some store windows. The streets are deserted at this hour.

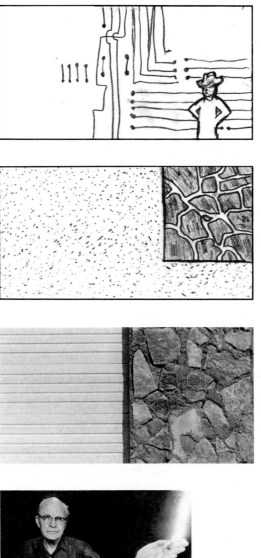

Jack Kilby, inventor of integrated circuit

Metal Buildings

Metal buildings are the dream that modern architects had at the beginning of the century come true, but they themselves don't realize it. If they followed their own theories to the letter—form follows function, using mass-production techniques to make cheap things with no frills—what you end up with is a metal building! And when you look at it that way, it's beautiful. The reason no architect ever says that is because you don't need an architect to build metal buildings. You order them out of a catalog. Just pick out your color, the size you want, number of square feet, style, and what you need it for. It comes with a bunch of guys, they put it together in a couple of days, maybe a week, and there you go. You're all set for business. Just stick a sign out front.

It takes people in a so-called uncultured or unsophisticated area like this to be open to the potentials of this kind of structure. For instance, people in the East tend to think that a bank has to be made of stone with columns out front, that a supermarket has to have lots of windows in front, that buildings have to have a structure that says what they are. It takes open-minded people to realize that all you have to do is slap a sign on a building to tell people what it is.

DB

NARRATOR (V.O.) Many of Virgil's festivities are sponsored by Varicorp. It's a major community-relations effort. They are calling it a "Celebration of Specialness" . . . But this place looks completely normal!

Photo of a Varicorp Building on the Flat Texas Landscape

In front of the image, which is now revealed to be a projection, we see a small figure . . . in front of the screen. His hair is short and neat, and he wears a Western-looking suit. It's the NARRATOR. *As he speaks, he sometimes glances over his shoulder at the big images as they change.*

NARRATOR This is the Varicorp plant, just outside Virgil. It's cool. It's sort of a multipurpose shape . . . a box.

End MUSIC

Exterior, Varicorp Plant—Early Morning

Complete Pull-Back to reveal the NARRATOR *and the photo of Varicorp which is projected onto a screen in a small lecture room.*

Interior, Varicorp Plant—(Day)

A LONG SLOW TRACKING SHOT *down the chip assembly line. We hear many overlapping conversations. The circuits are assembled on boards that move along as* WORKERS *on either side insert the components. All the workers wear pastel-colored coats to cover their own clothes.*

We see TWO GUYS *on the line grinning at each other . . . as if challenging each other.*

FIRST SMILER How's this for a Boston lady? Huh?

SECOND SMILER That's pathetic . . . mmm . . . Watch this, a sidewinder!

The CAMERA MOVES *on past them.* TWO TEENAGE GIRLS *are talking to each other.*

Texas Monthly

Behind the Lines
by Gregory Curtis

April 1984 Today farmers say they are going broke, the oil industry is stagnant, and steel plants are closing . . . No one expects oil to rebound. Its sudden fall inspired a frenzy of discussion about where we might find an industry to take oil's place as the prime mover in the economic life of Texas.

That discussion immediately centered on high tech . . . This industry is so new, potentially profitable, and squeaky clean that the mayors of our cities and the governor of our state plan to start programs both to attract new high-tech industries to Texas and to develop the ones that are already here . . .

There will be firms that choose to move to or expand in Texas simply because the real business of Texas is business. It holds the loftiest place in the imagination and values of the state and, finally, is the source of our greatest pride. We honor businessmen more than scientists or scholars, even more than doctors . . . Our most frequent source of self-congratulation is our healthy business climate and our can-do attitude . . .

But we should not be so infatuated with business that our strength becomes a weakness. The trouble with pinning too much hope on attracting companies to move here is that then they are the ones holding all the cards . . . They can pick and choose among the competing offers and play cities off one against the other . . .

Today the strengths of our economy are direct. We do basic things. We grow food and fiber; we find oil and refine it; we make things, like steel . . . Those industries tend to reward personal qualities like determination, force of will, and endurance for hard physical labor outdoors . . . They are industries in which working at one job, even the lowest, teaches you what you need to know to advance to the next job up the ladder. Yesterday's roughneck is today's tool pusher, and today's tool pusher may own a company tomorrow. As a result, Texas probably has more millionaires with gnarled, stubby fingers and weathered faces than any place else in the world.

A Texas dominated by high tech would be a very different place . . . The typical worker would have an ID clipped to his shirt rather than a hard hat on his head, and clean hands rather than dirty fingernails. Texas would look more like Plano than Fort Worth.

But the opportunities for advancement from the bottom would be severely curtailed. High tech values training more than raw will. Engineers and other white-collar workers form the top of a highly stratified industry pyramid that is not accessible through energy alone . . .

I'm not ready to lose that social mobility so easily or to transform Texas in the image of a silicon chip.

FIRST GIRL He's an asshole . . . I went out with him once . . . Nice car . . . Hey! You gonna come to the keg party at Don's tomorrow?

SECOND GIRL I think *both* of 'em are assholes . . . A real *attitude*, know what I mean?

NARRATOR'S VOICE (*off-screen*) But what about love?

On the assembly line the tracking shot has traveled down to where a WOMAN *with curly hair is working. She's about 33 years old and is obsessed with finding the beautiful or, in her word, "cute" in the world around her. It's a Hallmark-card world. She is attractive . . . but no knockout. Her fingers twitch as she talks.*

CUTE WOMAN Love makes everything look beautiful . . . like a little puppy! I like a hairy man. You know Jesus was hairy? . . . It's worth it to fall in love . . . to see the beautiful world . . . even though heartache is sure to follow.

She is overcome slightly by her vision and gently slips off her wheeled work chair to the floor.

The RHYTHM *of the* FACTORY LINE *continues as the* CAMERA MOVES *further down . . . another* WORKER *continues the discussion about love.*

WORKER Love is soft and love is pure.
Love is something that you must endure.
Love is peaceful and love is wild.
Love's alright if it lasts awhile!

On down the line a WOMAN *with a large hairdo smokes a cigarette as she takes this in. She speaks in an authoritative voice . . . telling obvious lies about herself.*

LYING WOMAN I know everything about love, honey. Seen it all . . . Done it all. I *love* money . . . and men like that. Remember when I went out with Burt Reynolds? He was *crazy* about me. He was ready to quit the movies and live with me. I said I needed all his money . . . He would'a given it to me, too. Men respect that.

Assembly Lines

New corporations whip these plants up really fast . . . stick 'em out there on the prairie. Just throw up a metal building in about a week or two and the employees seem to come from all over the country. Even Flint, Michigan, and Wooster, Mass; Wheeling, West Virginia, and Pittsburgh, PA. If you're lucky you can come down here, get a job in one of these places, be on the line real quick and, depending on your position, you can get a mobile home, single wide or double wide, as low as $26,000. Almost no money down. And that's just like these factories. You can stick your home anywhere. Stick it out there in the middle of the prairie. You're living in the country. You got a million-dollar view. You just left some Victorian-era smoke hole up in the Northeast.

The deal is making a fresh start. It's the best thing in the world. People don't want who they are to be confused with what they do. "Well, I work on the line at GM." But only for now. You can switch over and do something else when you feel like it, and live somewhere else and have new friends and be a completely different person. They don't know what you were like before. You could have been a total *drag.* You could have one kind of personality based on your relationships in one town. If you decide that isn't the best way to work things out, you could move to another town; be somebody else.

The CAMERA MOVES *on to a* HISPANIC
WORKER *whose dress seems a little more stylish,
or considered, than the others. He may even have
modified his work coat. He likes to flirt with the
ladies ... It may get obnoxious at times, but it adds
a little bit of fun to the day.*

RAMON   *(to the woman working next to him)* Look at
me ...

He stares at her very seriously.

RAMON   Now I'm going to lightly touch the bridge of
your nose ... don't be afraid.

WOMAN   What's this supposed to be?

RAMON   I can read your tones ... Everybody has tones.
Like a radio station. It's the music of your soul ...
it could be Cumbia or Rock or Easy Listening ...
Everybody is their own station ... a transmitter!

WOMAN   I guess you have your dial set?

RAMON   Baby! ... I'm the only one that's even got a
radio.

He moves closer to her.

RAMON   Now I'm picking you up. It's sort of cool ...
sort of hot.

RAMON *starts to groove to the imagined sounds
he hears. He* SNAPS *his fingers and sways to the*
RHYTHM *of the* ASSEMBLY LINE. *He rises out of
his chair and executes some overdramatic stage
gestures.*

He sings to the RHYTHM *of the* ASSEMBLY LINE,
*which has been building since the beginning of this
scene.*

RAMON   Baby your mind is a radio
The receiver is in my head
Baby I'm tuned to your wavelength
Lemme tell you what it says—

Transmitter!
Pickin' up something good
Hey radio head!
The sound—of a brand-new world

36

R.E.I. employees at Irving, Texas, 1985

RAMON   I'm going to rock the house on Friday night.

The CAMERA MOVES *past them. A* COMPUTER
ENGINEER *enters the* FRAME, *carrying some
parts. A guy that might once have been a hippie
but has now cleaned up enough to have employ-
ment at Varicorp ... Mainly because tinkering
with stuff, especially computers, is his passion.
Maybe he sees computers as some sort of tool that
will be of great assistance in the next phase of
human evolution.*

As the CAMERA APPROACHES *him, he turns and
speaks directly to it. The* CAMERA *then*
FOLLOWS *him as he moves around the plant.*

NARRATOR   I like it ... I like it ... I like it. Seems to be a
different attitude around here.

As he moves to another room, another SOUND *is
added ... almost musical.*

COMPUTER GUY   Yeah, something's happening here
all right ... The world is changing ... and this is
the center of it right now ... or one of many
centers.

It's a lot like music, know what I mean? ... I been
into music for a long time ... Computers are like
that ... You can never explain the connections or
feeling to anyone else.

Figuring something out ... something that's never
been understood before, is a rhythmic experience
... Steve Jobs said that, he used to be head of
Apple.

The COMPUTER GUY *sticks an* I.D. *card into a
door, which then opens, allowing the two of them
to enter the testing and acceptance room ... It is a
large, sterile-looking room filled with huge
machines.*

NARRATOR'S VOICE   You mean you like it here? This
is an exciting place to work, then?

COMPUTER GUY   Yeah ... I guess I'd say so. You
know, some people in the computer business can
be pretty creative, unlike the traditional business
person ... You know, the astronauts didn't read
poetry ... but that's changing ... Computers are as
much a medium of expression as language!

Texas Monthly

Birth of a New Frontier
by Harry Hurt III

April 1984 L. J. Sevin could pass for
an old-fashioned Texas wildcatter
... But Sevin doesn't drill for oil and
gas. He does his wildcatting in the
booming field of high technology.

"When you smell an opportunity,
you just can't turn your back on it,"
Sevin declares. "What's there, let's
face it, is greed—money."

Thanks to high-tech wildcatters
like L. J. Sevin ... Texas is the
fastest-growing high-tech center in
the nation ... The Dallas–Fort
Worth Metroplex, which has the
greatest concentration of high-tech
companies in the state, is often
referred to by the press and local PR
firms as Silicon Prairie. Central Texas
has been dubbed Silicon Hill Country, Silicon Gulch, and Silicon Cor-
ridor. Texas has become the high-
tech industry's new frontier ...

Governor Mark White campaigned
to bring MCC to Texas as if it were
the key to his reelection ... Bobby
Ray Inman, the ex-CIA deputy director who now heads MCC, believes
that high-tech development is vital to
our national security ...

At least forty Texas high-tech
companies have been founded or
funded by the former employees of
just two corporations: Collins Radio,
transplanted from Iowa, and Texas
Instruments.

What *is* high tech? The term has
been co-opted for so many uses in
so many fields—design, architecture, and even music, to name a
few—that purists like L. J. Sevin
have come to hate it. Today the term
usually refers to the vast array of
businesses that all rely upon the
same essential element: the silicon
chip.

The Bang Behind the Bucks
The Life Behind the Style

Steve Jobs on Status, Art, Ethics and the Future of the Personal Computer

by Tom Zito

Do you consider yourself the new astronaut, the new American hero?

No, no, no. I'm just a guy who probably should have been a semi-talented poet on the Left Bank. I got sort of sidetracked here. The space guys, the astronauts, were techies to start with. John Glenn didn't read Rimbaud, you know; but you talk to some of the people in the computer business now and they're very well grounded in the philosophical traditions of the last 100 years and the sociological traditions of the '60s. There's something going on here, there's something that is changing the world . . .

Do you think it's unfair that people out here in Silicon Valley are generally labeled nerds?

Of course. They're the people who would have been poets had they lived in the '60s. And they're looking at computers as their medium of expression rather than language . . .

I've noticed that an awful lot of those who work for you play music or are interested in it. Why music?

When you want to understand something that's never been understood before, what you have to do is construct a conceptual scaffolding. And if you're trying to design a computer you will literally immerse yourself in the thousands of details necessary; all of a sudden, as the scaffolding gets set up high enough, it will all become clearer and clearer and that's when the breakthrough starts. It is a rhythmic experience . . . everything's related to everything else and it's all intertwined . . . It's very much like music. But you could never describe it to anyone.

Playboy Interview:
Steven Jobs

A candid conversation about making computers, making mistakes and making millions with the young entrepreneur who sparked a business revolution

I met Jobs at a birthday party for a youngster in New York City. Jobs had gone off with the nine-year-old birthday boy to give him the gift he'd brought: a Macintosh computer. As I watched, he showed the boy how to sketch with the machine's graphics program.

Jobs stayed to tutor the boy on the fine points of using the Mac. Later, I asked him why. "Older people sit down and ask, 'What is it?' but the boy asks, 'What can I do with it?'"

Playboy: It's interesting that the computer field has made millionaires of guys like you and Steve Wozniak, working out of a garage ten years ago. What is this revolution you two seem to have started?

Jobs: We're living in the wake of the petrochemical revolution of 100 years ago. The petrochemical revolution gave us free energy—free mechanical energy, in this case. It changed the texture of society. This revolution, the information revolution, is a revolution of free energy as well, but of another kind: free intellectual energy. This revolution will dwarf the petrochemical revolution. We're on the forefront . . .

A computer is the most incredible tool we've ever seen. It can be a writing tool, a communications center, a supercalculator, a planner, a filer and an artistic instrument all in one, just by being given new instructions, or software, to work from . . .

People really don't have to understand how computers work. Most people have no concept of how an automatic transmission works, yet they know how to drive a car . . .

We think the Mac will sell zillions, but we didn't build Mac for anybody else. We built it for ourselves. We just wanted to build the best thing we could build. When you're a carpenter making a beautiful chest of drawers, you're not going to use a piece of plywood on the back, even though it faces the wall and nobody will ever see it . . .

Apple is an Ellis Island company. Apple is built on refugees from other companies. These are the extremely bright contributors who were troublemakers at other companies . . .

Everyone here has the sense that right now is one of those moments when we are influencing the future . . . We want to qualitatively change the way people work. We don't just want to help them do word processing faster or add numbers faster. We want to change the way they can communicate with one another . . . There's always been this myth that really neat, fun people at home all of a sudden have to become very dull and boring when they come in to work. It's simply not true.

I met Woz [Steve Wozniak] when I was 13. He was about 18. He was the first person I met who knew more electronics than I did . . . We also went into the blue-box business together. The famous story about the boxes is when Woz called the Vatican and told them he was Henry Kissinger. They had someone going to wake the Pope up in the middle of the night before they figured it out it wasn't really Kissinger . . .

When I went to college, every student in this country read *Be Here Now* and *Diet for a Small Planet*. *In Search of Excellence* [the book about business practices] has taken the place of *Be Here Now*.

Playboy: Did you and Wozniak have a vision once things started rolling?

Jobs: No, not particularly. Neither of us had any idea that this would go anywhere. Woz is motivated by figuring things out. He concentrated on the engineering. I was trying to find out what a company *was* . . .

Playboy: How did Silicon Valley come to be?

Jobs: Little by little, people started breaking off and forming competitive companies, like those flowers or weeds that scatter seeds in hundreds of directions when you blow on them. And that's why the Valley is here today . . .

We're making the largest investment of capital that humankind has ever made in weapons over the next five years. We have decided, as a society, that that's where we should put our money, and that raises the deficits and, thus, the cost of our capital. You get the feeling that the connections aren't made in America between things like building weapons and the fact that we might lose our semiconductor industry. We have to educate ourselves to that danger . . .

I think death is the most wonderful invention of life. It purges the system of these old models that are obsolete. There's an old Hindu saying that comes into my mind occasionally: "For the first 30 years of your life, you make your habits. For the last 30 years of your life, your habits make you."

. . . I think that Western rational thought is not an innate human characteristic. It is a learned ability. It had never occurred to me that if no one taught us how to think this way, we would not think this way.

Shot of a romance novel among the circuit boards

Interior, Varicorp—(Day)

Another Section of the Varicorp Plant

The Clean Room

It is large and spotless, in contrast to the almost funky atmosphere of the line. The few people in this room all wear white lab coats. The man near us, LOUIS FYNE, *is about 33 and slightly overweight. He has a pleasant face that is a little small for his head, which is almost square.*

He speaks to the camera.

LOUIS My name is Louis . . . Louis Fyne. I been working here a number of years . . . Now I work in the Clean Room . . . It's pretty O.K. I go out at night . . . I'm a dancin' fool . . . Hah!

Louis moves over and continues his work at one of the large pieces of equipment.

LOUIS I tell ya . . . I love the ladies . . . There's more to life than this job, no offense, you understand. I'm no swinger. Not Louis. I want to settle down and share. It would be beautiful. These machines are great . . . they're incredible . . . I tried a computer dating service once . . . wound up with a midget! . . . I'm not a fussy man, but hey!

Exterior, Louis Fyne's House—(Day)

There is a "wife wanted" sign in the yard . . . and a big heart in the window.

LOUIS (V.O.) I want someone to share my life . . . Marriage is a natural thing . . . and I'm a natural man . . . But these days it's frowned on . . . so I have to be direct.

Interior, Chinese Restaurant Dining Room—(Night)

Louis sits at a large round table surrounded by a WOMAN *and a* DOZEN KIDS . . . *This is obviously not what he had in mind.*

It's Me Magazine

Meet Mr. Wonderful

July/August 1984 I'm a single (never married) man who, for years now, has wanted all the joys and contentment of matrimony. Born in a world that prints a new "diet book" every month and considers the "average" girl or guy a "diet Pepsi girl" or "a Dannon yogurt guy"—my chances for someone looking at me for what I am, without judging my size, aren't too good. I'm 6'3", weigh 285 pounds (very consistently), and have a "panda bear" shape.

To be honest with you, I realized that there were women out there with the same problem as I, but who were assured and pleased about their state. I said to myself, "That's for me." I'm pleased with the way God made me, and wouldn't change anything about the way I am.

Weekly World News

Lonely Bachelor Hungers for Love
by Jack Alexander

Desperate bachelor Carl Dolan wants women to know he's a lonely heart looking for love. So he's planted seeds of matrimony—using "wife wanted" signs on his lawn and plopping a big red heart in his window . . .

"Single life is the pits," said lonesome Carl. "I want to settle down and share, not swing . . ."

"I'm getting a real complex," said the bearded 35-year-old . . . "There must be something about me that turns women off . . ."

Carl doesn't drink or smoke heavily, cooks a good chicken gumbo, and has a steady job . . . The romantic has spent hundreds of dollars wining, dining and dancing his way through evenings with 25 of the 450 women who've answered his "wife wanted" plea.

"I spent $600 to fly one woman to Boston. We wrote a bunch of letters and exchanged pictures. I thought she was Mrs. Right, but I was wrong," said Carl. "When I saw her she looked like a middle linebacker for the Pittsburgh Steelers. I said to myself, 'There's the beef . . .'"

"A couple of girls have driven by slowly, but they didn't stop," Carl sighed sadly, "They must think I'm a kook . . ."

His four matchmaking sisters are helping him aim for the right missus, but the blind dates they've found him have been disastrous . . .

"I fell head over heels for two of the women I've dated, but they got cold feet when the talk got down to marriage."

ML

LOUIS (V.O.)   I'm not fussy ... It's what's inside that counts ... But wait a minute! Gimme a break! ... My sister once introduced me to a friend of hers.

(Simultaneous dialogue)

WOMAN   Do you like children, Louis?

LOUIS   Are they arranged alphabetically?

KID #1   Where do you work?

KID #2   How much money do you make?

LOUIS   Oh ... a tidy sum ...

Interior, 60's Style Attic

Louis sits in a dark room surrounded by posters and piles of books. A WOMAN is attempting to teach him the lotus position ... He's having trouble keeping his balance on the waterbed.

LOUIS   I don't know, Moonstone ... What's the easiest yoga position?

WOMAN   The lotus, Louis ... Here, let me help you ...

Louis rocks over.

WOMAN   No, that's a different yoga position.

Interior, Car—Driving Through Town—Process Shot—(Day)

Obvious fake-looking shot ... although the images seen outside the fake windows are real Texas suburban towns. We see evidence of the various preparations being made for the sesquicentennial celebrations.

The NARRATOR is driving the car and talking to the camera.

NARRATOR   Well, I suppose these freeways made this town ... and many others ... possible. They're the cathedrals of our time. There are names for the various kinds of freeway drivers. The "slingshotter" ...

Flat Landscapes

When somebody says to you, "flat landscape," you might think it's something kind of bleak. But when you actually see it and you're in it and you're kind of experiencing it, it's really beautiful and majestic. It's not depressing at all. It's really inspiring.

People and things in flat landscapes are forced to be really honest because there's nothing to hide behind. People who grow up or live in this kind of environment are the first to accept themselves and other people for whatever it is they are, and to accept and love their quirks and eccentricities because they stick up. If somebody stands out there, they just kind of poke right up. If you can stand being like that, then you can stand just about anything.

A flat landscape is also a child's landscape. All a child needs to do to draw the horizon is draw a line across the middle of the paper. I noticed that some of my drawings as a child had something in common with the art of the Northwest American Indians. They are like X-rays or exploded views of the subject. If I drew people with clothes on, I drew what I knew was there. I knew they had a belly button and nipples so I'd put those things in there, showing right through their clothes. It didn't matter if your eye couldn't see them. You know they're there, so I put 'em right in. The people became kind of transparent.

ML

We see various vehicles zipping by the windows.

NARRATOR ... the "adventurer" ... the "marsh-mallow" ... the "nomad" ... the "weaver." It's fancy driving ... Things that never had names before now are easily described. It makes conversation easy ...

Outside, we see a large patch of flat land with some WORKERS *in the middle of it.* CUT *to a closer look at this site. Some equipment trucks are parked here and there ... a* GROUP *of very organized-looking* CHILDREN *watch from a distance. There is a large rectangle marked out on the ground in stakes and string.*

NARRATOR (V.O.) Now, here is where the stage for the performances is going to be built ... Should take a few days ... It's all prefab. Just in time, I hope ... Has anyone thought about parking? Huh?

Cut to: Exterior, Virgil Montage—(Day)

Various Views of Sections of the Town

Residential developments ... highways with honky-tonks. In the center of town, decorations are up and banners are run across the street. ''1836–1986 A CELEBRATION OF SPECIALNESS.''

NARRATOR (V.O.) These days, everyone gets ready. Have you seen that man before? Here's where the parade will run ... Do you like music? I know, everyone says they do, but liking things is not as easy as it seems.

Cut to: Interior, Car—(Dusk)

NARRATOR *in car*

Still driving around. It's TWILIGHT *now.*

NARRATOR Well, it's getting on ... Most people have eaten already. Don't want to be late, if you know what I mean ... or do you?

LJ

DB

The car pulls up to a CLUB *that is part of, or adjacent to, a shopping center or mall ... A series of low rectangular buildings surrounded by a huge parking lot.*

NARRATOR   You gotta see this ... It might be part of Virgil's Celebration of Specialness. Or it might not be ... Maybe you've seen it on TV ... Maybe you missed it ... but it's different here ... Hope you don't mind loud music ...

Cut to: Interior, Music Club—(Night)

Tables in the center, a bar to one side, and a stage up front ... backed by a wall of television sets, all with the same picture on them ... rock videos. Some people have stopped by who don't usually hang out here because of the event tonight ... so the audience is a mixture of regulars and strangers.

The Club D.J. *is off to the side. He brags and encourages the audience at the same time.*

M.C.   Welcome. Crazy Cajun talkin' to ya ... Good time, good music ... In a minute we got a song we all want you to lip-synch along with ... "Wild Wild Life," honey ... That's right, you be the star ... But hold on a minute, before you start getting stars in your eyes ... look at me. I'm cute ... Have my own band, money in the bank ... Wore out nine bodies, cars, alcohol ... three cars, three girlfriends, four wives, bunch of kids ... Look out, Michael Jackson ... If you've lost it, I don't need it. I'm livin', walkin', talkin' stereo video. Put one foot in front of the other ... You are the future in my video mind.

His rap continues in the background as we see other townspeople in the club.

We see LOUIS FYNE *sitting at the bar ... He's talking with a* WOMAN *as we approach.*

LOUIS   It's this drink where about six different kinds of liquor are mixed together ... see? But it don't taste too strong ... *(pause)* ... I'll bet you've seen me here before, huh? ... *Aarrgghhaaggaiaiaihh!! Rrraaggghhh! (roars like a bear)*

46

Twins

Twins confuse our ideas about individuality. We walk around thinking everybody is unique and then we see these two people who look like they're the same person and in subtle ways they kind of think alike and talk alike. I mean, granted, they are still individuals. They're not really the same person but they're more alike than we're used to thinking that two people can be. They demonstrate right in front of your eyes that individuality is in fact a choice in which something is lost, some kind of communication between people, an identity, part of a community. When we choose to accent and emphasize our individuality, we lose all these things.

ML

The Narrator walks up, attracted by Louis' roar.

LOUIS   I'm the *dancing* bear ... *(turns to the* NARRATOR*)* Ain't that right?

NARRATOR   Hi, Louis. How you doin'? ... You gonna dance on Friday?

Louis motions to the narrator as if he wants to say something confidential ... They ease away.

LOUIS   Yeah ... Yeah ... I'm working on my song ... But! ... *(whispers)* ... I'm still having a hard time with the ladies ... Buddy! ... I'll tell ya!

We see various WOMEN *in the Club as* LOUIS' *voice-over continues ... we see the* LYING WOMAN *chatting up a* MAN *at the bar.*

LYING WOMAN   I'm a personal friend of Sly ... I met him in Hollywood on a business trip at a roller-skating rink ... He was watching me do my figure skating ... He's been trying real hard to get a correspondence going between us ... I don't give a diddly squat for him.

Louis and the narrator walk through the club.

LOUIS   *Fact:* There are a half-million more single guys than gals ... Competition is tough ... And most of them want to swing or aren't really serious ... Some of these gals are as bad as the guys!

They sit down and the WAITER *brings drinks.*

NARRATOR   The green one's mine.

LOUIS   I'll take the other one. Hey, listen to this that I read ...

Meanwhile, the Lying Woman continues.

LYING WOMAN   When I was a nurse in Vietnam I was stuck out in the middle of the jungle with the real Rambo. He had the hots for me ... He nearly drove me crazy ... Course, it would be very difficult for a person not to fall in love with you out there in that humidity ... I saved his life about 50 times. I was highly decorated ... He was good-looking, too. He was cuter than Sly.

ML

Cut to: KAY, *selling raffle tickets, is the wife of* EARL CULVER, *a respected Civic Leader in Virgil. From her posture we can assume that she is here in a semiofficial capacity. Her arms are crossed, but she's enjoying the scene.*

RAMON *has just approached* LOUIS. *He is dressed a little more casually now ... but with quite a bit of flair.*

RAMON   Hey, Louis! Want me to read your tones?

He touches Louis' nose and closes his eyes, trance-like. Ramon shakes his head at the confusion of signals he is receiving. He makes a face ... then LAUGHS.

RAMON   Wooo! ... Hey, man, don't worry about it. Louis, you're alright.

LYING WOMAN   I love my trips, though ... I guaran—damn—tee ya. I just work at Varicorp for a hobby.

MUSIC *in the club has been building throughout. Now, however, everyone's attention turns to the little stage, as various members of the audience step up and lip-synch to a new* TALKING HEADS SONG *that the* D.J. *is playing.*

Each person's interpretation of the song is different, and it is amazing to watch the transformations take place as various WORKERS, *etc., "put on" another personality or reveal their own. The song itself becomes a vehicle that can say anything they want it to. Some gestures and movements are obviously derived from well-known sources: television shows ... movies ... and, most recently, rock videos.*

Odd to think that some lip-synchers are imitating characters in Videos, who are really musicians imitating other characters.

Other lip-synchers have come up with completely original styles and moves ... or overlay one style with a series of gestures from another, completely different, style.

The New York Times

Shopping Malls Become Stages for Mimed Music
by Clifford D. May

November 8, 1985 "Now listen, I don't want any booing," said Diane Schoenbaum, taking the microphone and addressing the audience in Sunrise Mall near the Plaza Dental Group, the Candy Castle, and Buster Brown Shoes.

The audience murmured its consent while the performers milled about nervously.

Finally the first act mounted the makeshift stage. Three girls, aged 14 to 15, launched into "Hanky Panky," singing up a storm.

Or more precisely, giving the appearance of singing up a storm. For all the entertainers in the mall were "lip sync" and "air band" artists, skilled in providing the illusion that they were singing or were playing musical instruments.

Musical miming has emerged as a hot performing art in the suburbs. "Tons of bars and colleges have lip-sync and air-band contests," said Miss Schoenbaum, producer of the Sunrise Mall extravaganza. "It's very popular."

. . . The shopping mall is the natural venue for such an event because in the suburbs the mall has become the equivalent of the village square . . .

"I've competed in clubs here on the Island, in Westchester, and in Connecticut," said Jon Bass, 22. "I've won loads of times."

Mr. Bass, who was dressed in tribute to the rock singer Adam Ant, replete with pony tail, polka dot revolver, dangling earring and war paint, claimed some expertise on the subject.

"What really promotes it are all the rock videos on TV," he said. "You watch those videos, and you want to do it, to play it out. And actually all they're doing in those videos is lip syncing anyhow."

. . . Although malls tend to look alike, different malls in different kinds of neighborhoods attract contestants with assorted tastes.

"Like, in Brooklyn you get a lot of break dancing and rapping," said Mr. Bass. "Or you go to Levittown, you might get punk. And in Connecticut there's more, like, commercial New Wave."

. . . At the Sunrise Mall, there were ersatz Elvises, mock Madonnas, make-believe Michael Jacksons, bogus Bruce Springsteens, proxy Pointer Sisters, simulated Cyndi Laupers and even a sham Sha Na Na . . .

[One participant] had done herself up convincingly as Mr. T. "I'm a big ham," she said. And no stranger to show business either: "I used to be a mud wrestler."

. . . At the end of the Sunrise Mall contest, the first prize went to Samantha O'Brien, who gave a spirited performance in the guise of Madonna. Miss O'Brien, who is 6 years old and hopes to become a veterinarian someday, received an ovation so thundering it might well have been audible clear over at the Busy Bee Mall on the other side of Sunrise Highway.

When all that positive clapping and cheering finally died down, Miss O'Brien was asked how she felt about winning. She smiled brightly and opened her mouth to speak. Appropriately, not a word came out.

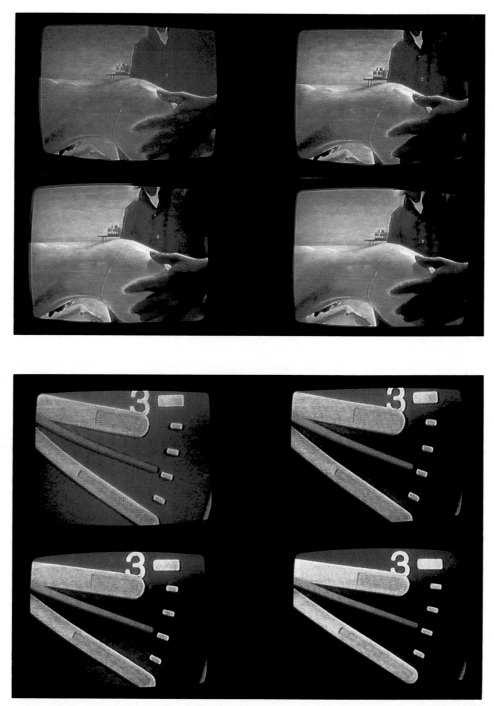

EL

A LARGE WOMAN *does a sexy interpretation of the song . . . which has few sexual references. She is an inspiration, totally unashamed of her size . . . She makes us forget it as well.*

A MAN *lip-synchs, using gestures which seem to have no obvious show-business references . . .*

The COMPUTER GUY *from the plant identifies more with the instrumental sections of the song than the lyrics or singing. He moves his mouth and face in an effort to express the musical sounds . . . facial expressions in sympathy with the notes and textures.*

LOUIS FYNE *himself interprets a portion of the song. He injects all the deep intensity of his search for a mate into his performance. It is an expression of inappropriately genuine emotion. It is touching to see this in the midst of this Club scene.*

A TEENAGER *plays Heavy Metal Air Guitar and screws up his face.*

RAMON *shows off some more of his original dramatic stage moves. He spins for a minute like a dervish. He's the most energetic performer we see . . . a style perfectly suited to lip-synching, as one could never sing and move like this at the same time.*

SONG   I'm wearin'/Fur pyjamas
                I ride a/Hot potata'
                It's tickling my fancy
                Speak up, I can't hear you

1ST CHORUS   Here on this mountaintop
                Woahoho
                I got some wild, wild life
                I got some news to tell ya,
                Woahoho
                About some wild, wild life
                Here comes the doctor in charge
                Woahoho
                She's got some wild, wild life
                Ain't that the way you like it?
                Ho, ha!
                Living wild, wild life.

                I wrestle, with your conscience
                You wrestle, with your partner
                Sittin' on a window sill, but he
                Spends time behind closed doors

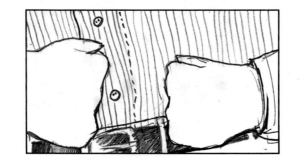

ML

2ND CHORUS Check out Mr. Businessman
Oh, ho ho
He bought some wild, wild life
On the way to the stock exchange
Oh, ho ho
He got some wild, wild life
Break it up when he opens the door
Whoahoho
He's doin' wild, wild life
I know that's the way you like it.
Wo ho
Living wild, wild life.

Peace of mind?
Piece of cake!
Thought control!
You get on board anytime you like

(Guitar Solo)

Like sittin' on pins and needles
Things fall apart, it's scientific

3RD CHORUS Sleeping on the interstate
Woah ho ah
Getting wild, wild life
Checkin' in, a checkin' out!
Uh, huh!
I got a wild, wild life
Spending all of my money and time.
Oh, ho ho
Done too much wild, wild
We wanna go, where we go, where we go
Oh, ho ho!
I doing wild, wild
I know it, that's how we start
Uh, huh
Got some wild, wild life
Take a picture, here in the daylight
Oh, ho!
And it's a wild, wild life
You've grown so tall, you've grown so fast
Oh, ho ho
Wild, wild
I know that's the way you like it
Oh, ho!
Living wild wild wild wild, life.

Cut to: Exterior, Virgil Montage—(Night)

Various Nighttime Scenes—as Virgil Goes to Bed

Lights are going out in a house (Cute Woman's House).

A JANITOR *is cleaning an office building or Varicorp.*

TWO KIDS *being given a drunk test by* POLICE *in front of a 7–11 store. One walks backward with his arms outstretched, and the other, with his eyes closed, slowly attempts to touch the tip of his nose with his finger.*

The SOUND *of the little girl from Scene One . . . a* DOG *crosses the street.*

Clouds pass across the moon.

Exterior, Cute Woman's House—(Night)

A typical suburban tract house, except that, like many of the buildings in Virgil, this one also seems to be surrounded by vast empty space. A few concrete animals and lawn decorations are out front.

Soft atmospheric MUSIC *as we pick out the* SOUND *of a* VOICE *. . . mumbling words and phrases . . . almost an incantation.*

CUTE WOMAN (V.O.) Is the world . . . seeing . . . getting? . . . cuter or uglier? . . . no . . . no . . . I'll look at that! . . . with my little eyes . . . Cleaning is looking with beautiful eyes . . . Why not? . . . If everyone could see like I do . . . Hello? . . . That's a nice tie you have on . . .

Interior Bedroom—(Night)

MUSIC *continues. We are looking down on the bed, which is lit by lights which illuminate the bed and nothing else. In fact, they illuminate it so brightly that it becomes an intense, glowing rectangle . . . with a* VOICE *emanating from it.*

The CAMERA *begins to move down, closer to the source of the sound, as the voice continues:*

Edgecliff, Texas

CUTE WOMAN (V.O.) If I were a flower and you were a leaf. There would be bears on every branch. If love has a message, then what a relief. To return the favor, with only a glance. Aahh! ... *(sighs)*

As the CAMERA *moves closer to the bed, subtle changes take place in the lighting. The lights from passing cars pass across the walls and bed. And the intensity of the illumination on the bed lowers, allowing us now to see the form of the* CUTE WOMAN *talking in her sleep as we continue to move toward her at a steady rate.*

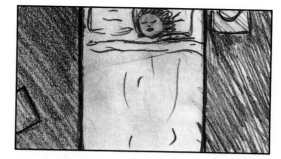 

CUTE WOMAN (V.O) It might be the water ... here are the talented people ... So many of them! ... Excuse me, are you from Virgil, Texas? Who are those people on the hills ... Angels! ... Little Angels ... Have you come to celebrate with us, my dears? Ow! ... Oops! ... I didn't mean to bump you.

The CAMERA *is much closer now. The Cute Woman's talking head fills the screen and the light has continued to dim, to normal exposure.*

CUTE WOMAN Let me count you all ... why! ... you're the years of my life ... I remember 7 ... seven's a lucky number! ... thirteen was the year ... Fourteen, angels here! ... 20, worked at home ... 21 ... Love has gone ... 22 ... There is another ... But he becomes a soldier ... 23 is like a painting ... 24 ... I'm still waiting ...

We are now so close to her that her moving mouth fills the screen ... and the light has slowly become a DEEP BLUE.

CUTE WOMAN ...Here's the music ... Who are those men over there? ... There's a cute one ... I'm a cute one ...

The Cute Woman's voice FADES OUT ...

Various Shots of Virgil—Asleep—Bits of Town

A couple of lights on here and there ... the flat landscape at night ... the SOUND *of* CRICKETS *... a* CAR ZOOMS *by.*

Blackout. MUSIC *stops.*

ML

Exterior, Virgil—(Daybreak)

A sunrise over the flat landscape . . . BIRDS SING-
ING . . .

Stage Construction Site

*Some scaffolding is up now on the site we drove by
earlier . . . A* NIGHT WATCHMAN *sits on a folding
chair and watches a television which is propped up
on the open back of a station wagon.*

Exterior, The Lazy Woman's House—(Day)

*On a sizable piece of land. This is the first shot of
this sequence in which the* CAMERA *begins to
move toward the object of interest. We see an old
van, painted with mystic symbols, parked
alongside the house.*

As we continue to move closer we HEAR *a* VOICE:

LAZY WOMAN (V.O.)   Reruns! Robert . . . look at this
. . . This remote thing isn't getting all the channels
. . . I don't want to miss that foolishness on Friday
. . . Get it fixed immediately.

MR. ROBERT TUCKER   Oh, yeah. I know a young man
who can fix that, no problem . . . Do you want that
old black-and-white TV? This young man would
really appreciate it.

*Cut to: Interior, the Lazy Woman's Bedroom—
(Day)*

MISS ROLLINGS, *the Laziest Woman in the
World, is in bed watching* TV. *She is surrounded
by various gadgets which enable her to do almost
anything she wants without leaving bed. Remote-
control television, speaker phone, various invalid
trays and hospital exercise devices . . . and a bed
that inclines itself at the push of a button. She is
about 40 years old, with a surprisingly energetic
personality for someone who has decided to spend
all her time in bed. As she talks she uses an automatic page turner to leaf through a magazine for
her while she does her nails. Her assistant,* MR.
TUCKER, *is a black man in his 50's with a very
calm, serene demeanor.*

LJ

60

LJ

LAZY WOMAN   I'd completely forgotten about that thing! ... If I ever went downstairs I might be surprised, huh? ... *Ha!* ... It's clean down there, isn't it, Roberto? That girl does a good job, doesn't she?

MR. TUCKER   It's so clean it scares me. You know you have the beauty operator coming later?

LAZY WOMAN   Yep ... Hey! ... How should I do it this time? Should I have it moussed?

She fluffs up her hair ... then points to something on the television.

LAZY WOMAN   There's a look! What do you think of that look? ... How about the gals in this show?

MR. TUCKER   These people have too much metal on them, Miss Rollings. They are a reflecting kind of people.

LAZY WOMAN   Yeah, you're right. But what do you think? ... Do they look that way because they're from Los Angeles, *or* do they think that's what we want to see? ... *or* ... Does the television do it to them?

MR. TUCKER   Whatever you think is what you get, Miss Rollings.

LAZY WOMAN   Speaking of get ... How're those shares of Varicorp doing ... *(pause; looks at him for an answer)*

MR. TUCKER   Oh, about 40 or 50 thousand ...

LAZY WOMAN   ... Is that all? Well, I'm not surprised ... Cheap bastards ... It's all the same all over, I guess ... Bunch a maniacs out there ... Wooo!

You know how hot dogs come 10 to a pack ... and buns in packs of 8 or 12 ... you have to buy 9 packs to make them match up ... That's what I'm talking about!

MR. TUCKER   That is the positive inside the negative. That is the outside world, Miss Rollings. *(pause)* That lawyer's coming over tomorrow ...

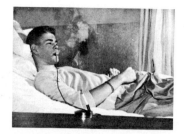

Smoker's robot

Peg extension handle for grooming

Click card holder

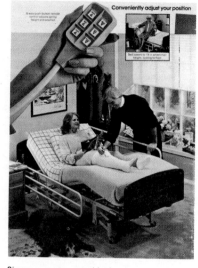

Six-way remote control bed
Sears Home Health-Care Specialog

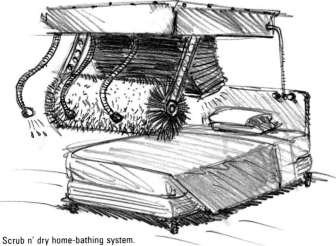

Scrub n' dry home-bathing system.

"Front only" clothes—she never gets up, so no need for back side.

The Wall Street Journal

Why Do Hot Dogs Come in Packs of 10 And Buns in 8s or 12s?

Often with these questions, the reply's just because; as for Oreos, don't ask.

by John Koten

September 21, 1984 The Nabisco Brands Inc. executive put her foot down.

"We can't tell you something like that," she snapped. "That's all highly confidential information."

The question the snack-foods executive had been asked: Why do Oreo cookies come 42 to a pack?

As the incident demonstrates, the dark secrets of packaging aren't always easy to unwrap . . . The issue also can be fraught with complexities.

What else would explain why hot dogs come in packages of 10 while hot-dog buns come in bags of eight or 12?

. . . Among the giants of marketing, decisions on such weighty issues can take on all the intensity of a religious debate. A former Procter & Gamble Co. manager, for instance, says that during his tenure the company was in an almost constant state of agony over how many paper towels it should put on a roll of Bounty.

"We couldn't decide if we should try to make each sheet big enough to handle the average-sized spill or whether we should assume most users tear off more than one sheet at a time."

Bohemia beer lowered the quantity in each bottle to 11 ounces from the standard 12. They then applied some of the cost savings toward a fancier container and a bigger ad budget. Sales nearly doubled . . .

Campbell Soup Co. believes it is better off selling its pork and beans in a 20¾ ounce can, while rival Stokely–Van Camp Inc. merrily goes on selling its brand in 21-ounce cans.

When Kimberly-Clark Corp. recently brought out a new version of Kleenex, its marketing experts had little doubt that the company should put 60 tissues in each pack. Why? "Because that's the average number of times people blow their nose during a cold."

Sometimes the consumer seems just plain irrational. Oscar Mayer & Co. says it routinely gets complaints from customers who want hot dogs sold in packs of eight or 12 to match the number of buns they get to a bag. But an official laments that whenever the company has tried to comply by selling wieners in those quantities, hardly anyone has bought them. "We can't explain it," he says with a sigh . . .

Regional preferences also can affect the popularity of a size. In the toilet-paper business, there is a trade-off between the thickness of sheets and the number on a roll. "Californians go for more sheets. Southerners like thicker sheets."

A candy-bar maker has decided never to put more than one piece of chocolate in a pack because "people secretly hate to share their candy with someone else."

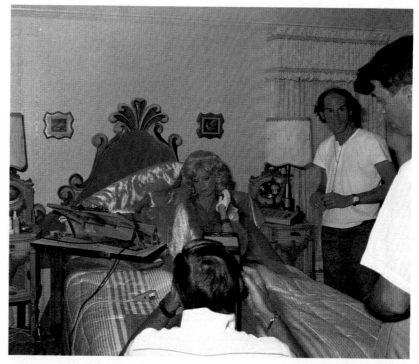

64

LJ

ML

LAZY WOMAN   Yeah ... well ... I'll outlive *him* anyway.

She reaches over to one of her labor-saving devices and puts it in motion.

Mr. Tucker holds up photos from a magazine.

MR. TUCKER   Miss Rollings, do you like this one? How about this person?

LAZY WOMAN   Good teeth ... Hi there ...

Cut to: Exterior, Stage Construction Site—(Day)

The scaffolding framework has grown. It now forms a box shape in the middle of the plain. TWO WORKERS *tell each other jokes.*

WORKER #1   These nuns were walking in the woods ... An Irishman, a Scotsman, and a Jew ... and this one says ...

A GROUP *of* CHILDREN *run by in single file.*

WORKER #2   This guy walks up to a girl in a bar and says ...

A GROUP *of* WORKERS *move* INTO FRAME ... *Moving in an ordered fashion. The* SOUNDS *of* CONSTRUCTION *in the background make a noisy but definite rhythm. The work goes on to the beat.*

WORKER #1   This guy had a lot of money, right? ... And the other guy farts real loud ...

WORKER #2   ... And whenever the gal saw it ... she would say ... in a real high voice ...

The "Chuck Wagon" mobile fast-food truck pulls into the site and stops.

WORKER #2   Lunch time! A celebration of sandwiches!

All of them drop what they're doing and head for the food truck.

LJ

Cut to: Exterior, Shopping Mall—(Day)

A low structure in the middle of a vast parking lot, beyond which we can see the flat landscape and the enormous sky.

The NARRATOR *is in the parking lot, talking directly to the* CAMERA.

NARRATOR   Since this mall opened, C.R. Anthony, J.C. Penney, and Duke and Ayres have all pulled out of "downtown." Gibsons, right on the corner, went under. I guess people really don't care whether they buy their stuff in funky old buildings or in a place like this. They're wise to advertisers' claims. In a place like this they can comparison-shop.

MARGIE *(off-screen)*   Everybody could hardly wait until the mall opened.

NARRATOR   Said Margie Ortiz.

MARGIE *(enters frame)*   I go there just about every weekend. So do two of the other gals at work.

NARRATOR   That's exactly what I'm talking about. See, I told ya.

Cut to: Interior, Shopping Mall—(Day)

A "street" of enclosed shops extends into the distance. PEOPLE *mill about and stare into the shop windows ... there is no really outstanding architecture, no distracting design elements ... but there are some banners and signs for the "Celebration of Specialness."*

The Narrator walks through the mall, weaving around the SHOPPERS *as the* CAMERA *follows. Background* SOUNDS *and* VOICES FADE IN AND OUT.

NARRATOR   The shopping mall has replaced the town square as the center of many American cities. "Shopping" has become the thing that brings people together.

The music is always playing here.

Outlet Mall, McKinney, Texas

68

Mall, Big Town, Texas

DB

The CAMERA *moves to a* PASSERBY, *who speaks to a friend.*

PASSERBY   Why, you couldn't carry a tune in a bucket with the lid hammered down.

NARRATOR   What time is it? No time to look back.

The CAMERA *moves over to a drugstore, where we see* TWO TEENAGERS *looking at tabloids and magazines in a rack. They stand, evenly spaced, and read quotes to one another.*

TEENAGER #2   "His experience with drugs taught him a lesson."

TEENAGER #1   "She turned to God when her breasts fell."

TEENAGER #1   "Baby born with two heads!" "Starving peasants surrender their bodies to greedy vampires for blood money!"

TEENAGER #2   "Aerobics craze injures 3 out of 4 instructors!" "We're being invaded by kangaroos from outer space!"

TEENAGER #1   "Granny guns down grandpa, stuffs him in closet!"

TEENAGER #2   "Three good ways to tell your love is over—three bad ways!" "Scientists baffled by pink vapor in 1,000-year-old flask, genie arises from bottle!" ... Maybe it was Barbara Eden! "Boy whose earmuffs took world by storm!"

TEENAGER #1   "He tried to sell vacuum cleaners door to door but was a huge flop!" "Why England's ex-king was drummed out of royal circles!"

TEENAGER #2   "Tunnel of death claims 4 lives, train ride to oblivion!" "Can you turn these pages into Xmas ornaments?"

TEENAGER #1   "Look what happens when you rest!" "We're being invaded by kangaroos from outer space!"

They double over LAUGHING *at what they're reading as the* CAMERA *moves on.*

Shopping Mall, Plano, Texas   LJ

Plano, Texas   LJ

Texas Monthly

Wal-Marts Across Texas

Small towns like Mount Pleasant, Hondo, and Aransas Pass are being invaded by a billion-dollar five-and-ten. And they love it.

by Rod Davis

October 1983 The best thing about Hondo is the welcoming sign, "This is God's Country, Please Don't Drive Through It Like Hell," but the newest thing on the horizon is the Wal-Mart on Texas Highway 90. Bright and snappy, 40,000 square feet of panache, the Wal-Mart is a cathedral dedicated to the great names of modern civilization—WD-40, Black & Decker, Rubbermaid, WaterPik, d-Con, Coleman . . .

There are now dozens of discount chains. But there has never before been anything like Wal-Mart. At the Wal-Mart in Aransas Pass, a California woman stood next to me in a shopping line. "It's just like this at all these stores. It's got to where you can go across the country and everything looks the same."

. . . Wal-Mart is not merely a business but a system of organization, living, and thought. The chain's nearly 60,000 workers are not employees but "associates," motivated by rewards for performance. Employees get a percentage of the store's savings and may participate in stock purchases.

The company magazine, *Wal-Mart World*, is filled with articles about employee enthusiasm, and some outlets even boast cheerleading squads.

Wal-Mart! Wal-Mart! That's our name!
The retailing business is our game!
We've got what it takes to be number one!
So watch out K Mart! Here we come!

Wal-Mart is about value . . . So-called upscale stores and manufacturers contort or disguise real value. They try to convince shoppers, through advertising, that the value of items is multiplied many times over by their association with illusions of status. Shoppers get confused and pay dearly for the brilliant subterfuge around an object. Wal-Mart is for people who see things as they are . . .

Another way of looking at Wal-Mart is from the cool, century-old, wooden, pigeonholed stock shelves in the back room at Luhn & Johns Rexall Drug Store in downtown Taylor. "What's it doing?" says pharmacist Bill Haase about Wal-Mart. "It's killing us."

Banker Ed Griffith of City National is also worried. "Just take a look out on Main Street," he snaps, gesturing toward the vacant stores there . . . Few businesses have taken their places and lasted. Wal-Mart *is* disruptive; its target cities are characterized by the disruption of population expansion, new industry, and new money . . .

It makes little difference to the residents of Taylor whether they buy their goods in funky old buildings or clean new prefabs, unless prices and selection are better at one place than another. And residents know where they're better. "Before Wal-Mart came here," said a cafe owner, "those stores downtown never heard of a sale."

Texas Monthly

Post-Modern Times

NorthPark dared to be different. It dared to be good.

by Michael Ennis

November 1985 Raymond D. Nasher's vision sits beneath him at the intersection of Park Lane and Central Expressway in Dallas, one of those mixed-use small complexes that is more than a collection of stores; it's a full-fledged "urban node." There is a kind of ceremoniousness to the structure that makes it easy to imagine the complex as a ruin; the great, pillared entrances lead not to halls echoing with the immortal footsteps of pharaohs and caesars but to the trade routes of the mighty American consumer . . .

The mall age as we know it today, for Dallas and for the world, really began back in 1960 . . . Nasher followed the same line of thinking as the other mall seers: the automobile would determine the movement of Americans . . . and the roads they traveled would lead away from Rome, away from the city center. But Nasher believed that a mall should be the nucleus of something that could eventually rival the great city centers of the Old World. The roads were leading away from Rome, so move Rome . . .

NorthPark has remained competitive in a young mall's game. There have been changes. There's Sunday afternoon family shopping; judging from the number of be-suited heads-of-households, malling is going to be a big post-church pastime. Nasher looks at today's NorthPark as a center of culture. He has decked the mall with museum-quality modern sculpture and introduced live chamber music. "What you're trying to create here is almost a university," he says. "You're trying to create an alumnus instead of a consumer. If you don't create an alumni association, then those consumers will be here today and gone tomorrow."

The New York Times Book Review

Cathedrals of Consumption

**The Malling of America
An Inside Look at the Great Consumer Paradise
by William Severini Kowinski**

By Grady Clay

February 17, 1985 Since World War II in North America, concentrations of capital spilled out along new federally subsidized highways, covered old countryside with a new suburbia and concentrated around interchanges. And there we find the profitable new malls . . .

In the good old days, "all the things that made a community happened on Main Street." But now, downtown had lost its heart. "Everything that was happening was happening on the [new] mall." Shopping had become the chief cultural activity in "our united states of shopping."

. . . These new malls had their own rules and private police to enforce them. The theme behind their design and management was a three-part principle: enclosure, protection and control . . . No room here for bare-bones bargains, independent merchants—or for groceries. No tolerance at these malls for noise, political rallies, or petitioners to disturb the shoppers' fixation on fashions and trademarks . . .

Malls and television reinforced each other by preprogramming the Baby Boom generation to get on with the great American pastime, "earning their wings as junior consumers," sharing shopping dates and the thrills of buying . . . What television proposed, the mall disposed. Then came video cassettes to complete the mall-television-video-fashion cycle.

Cut to: A kid passes by, humming to herself the tune of a well-known commercial jingle.

NARRATOR   The shops are clean. They're fairly new ... Not hard to find. Plenty of parking.

We see the COMPUTER GUY *from the Varicorp plant walking out of a "Computerland" or "Radio Shack" store with loads of equipment in his arms. His clothes are more casual now, and he has a few days' growth of beard.*

COMPUTER GUY   Hi.

NARRATOR   Hi ... How come you're not at work?

COMPUTER GUY   Oh ... I'm working on a project at home.

NARRATOR   What're you gonna do with all this stuff?

COMPUTER GUY   I send signals up.

NARRATOR   Oh, you mean, satellites.

COMPUTER GUY   Further than that, I hope. Listen. Do you believe that there are other forms of intelligent life in outer space?

NARRATOR   Well, I think it's possible, I guess ... But I don't think they are angels ... I think they're just as messed up as we are ...

COMPUTER GUY   Possible! ... It's a statistical certainty ... I just don't know where ...

NARRATOR   Oh, so *that's* what all this stuff is for ...

COMPUTER GUY   Hey. I gotta get back to work ... Before all hell breaks loose ... see ya!

NARRATOR   I hope so.

Cut to: GROUP *of* PEOPLE *in identical lodge or club outfits.*

ML

NARRATOR It's great how everyone has their own private system of belief. Originality. Creating it.

We see or overhear PEOPLE SINGING *or* HUMMING *lines from commercial jingles …* "You deserve a break today" … "The Jordache Look" … "I'm a Pepper, you're a Pepper."

Doing it … Selling it … Driving … not only driving but parking … Making it up as they go along. Experiencing it.

A MAN *admonishes his* GRANDCHILD: You can tell I'm not fooling when my lips aren't moving.

NARRATOR (V.O.) Hey! … There's Louis .

The CAMERA SWINGS AROUND *and* LOUIS *stops to chat.*

NARRATOR Hey … What's up? … Did you meet anyone at the club last night?

LOUIS Nah … They're all too wild … but I had a good time anyway.

We see a GROUP *of* TEENAGERS *teasing one another. Poking.* LAUGHING.

The CAMERA PANS *to a group of* SENIOR CITIZENS *doing exactly the same thing.*

NARRATOR So … What are you doing here? … What are you shopping for? … Or are you just hanging out?

LOUIS Oh … Just looking around … Thought I'd check out the fashion show down there … It's part of the Celebration … Maybe I'll pick up a few tips. You know I'm very aware of my appearance … Check these out …

Louis points to his shoes. A pair of very scientific-looking shoes … they were probably pretty expensive. Then he and the Narrator look up and see:

TWO BABIES *on the floor in front of several video monitors with a Lucky Charms commercial on. They are playing. They make* SOUNDS *which make the channel change to a Miller Lite commercial.*

Shopping Malls

You learn so much in a shopping mall and it's fun too. You can find out what everybody's thinking about, what they're dressing like, how they spend their leisure time, what they think is important, what they think is funny. You don't need to run all over the place to find out what's going on. One trip through the mall and you're up to date. If I was a politician, I would spend most of my time in malls. Just from looking at the clothing on the racks you can tell what people's political inclinations are.

Northpark Mall, Dallas

LOUIS   Like the song says, "It's a scientific lifestyle" ... *Woah*!

We see what LOUIS *is looking at ... At this end of the mall a* STAGE *and* RUNWAY *have been set up. It's for the Fashion Show, which has just begun. Louis is right, there seem to be* WOMEN *everywhere, sitting in folding chairs and just milling about.*

A podium is on the left, where a WOMAN *is talking. A small musical* COMBO *is below stage level on the right. A deep red curtain covers the whole of the back, so the backstage preparations and the rest of the Mall are hidden from us.*

LOUIS   This place is filled with women! That's Kay Culver ... She's married to Earl ... You've heard of him? *Well* ... he pretty much singlehandedly brought Varicorp to Virgil ... You know, I'll bet this mall wouldn't be here if it weren't for him.

NARRATOR   Oh, yeah? ... I'm going to have dinner with them later.

LOUIS   Well, listen ... I heard that Earl and Kay haven't spoken to one another in years ... at least not directly. Can you believe it?

NARRATOR   But she has such a beautiful voice.

KAY *extends her arm in a sweeping gesture that introduces the Fashion Show.*

KAY CULVER   Good afternoon, ladies and gentlemen. Welcome to another lovely event for the Celebration of Specialness. I think you'll be seeing a lot of new things today, and remember, you saw them here first ... Look for all these creations in the stores next month.

The curtains part and a group of models dressed like BUSINESS PEOPLE *appear in a wedge of the runway.*

KAY CULVER   Also let me remind you about the Talent Show, which is also part of the Celebration of Specialness, on Friday night at 8 P.M. under the stars.

Fashion Shows

One year I went to a lot of fashion shows. Did you know that they make special versions of the clothes for the tall skinny girls in fashion shows and they never even sell those versions? The ones they sell to the public are completely different. It doesn't matter. Most of the clothes you see on the runways are just a little bit more outrageous than anything you'd want to wear in your daily life anyway.

In the middle of one fashion show I went to, these women came out in their underwear. They were modeling bras and panties and they were carrying teddy bears. Whatever kinds of clothes are out there, you'd best believe there's a fashion show for them. They have fashion shows for farmers' clothes. Somebody has to come and see what the new style looks like if they want to buy it for all the stores. So there has to be a show. Police uniforms. Outfits for people who work in doughnut shops. It's all got to be presented in a dramatic, theatrical way.

What they are really selling, though, is not the physical garment, it's a state of mind. It's a mood. It's a way of feeling. People would like to be able to buy a way of feeling. They sure don't need another *shmatte* in the closet.

ML

She gives directions to the stage as the models move down the runway. KAY *looks at her watch and the models look at their watches as she speaks.*

KAY CULVER What time is it? If everyone notices ... Maybe it's too much ... But where would we be?

The BUSINESS PEOPLE *disappear as the next group comes out—* UNIFORM PEOPLE *(4 guys in yellow slickers followed by 4 waitresses, followed by 4 construction workers, followed by 4 `Girl and Boy-Scout leaders).*

KAY $29.95 is a pretty good price. With six outfits and as many combinations. The possibilities are endless. Shopping is a feeling!

The MUSIC *begins (*INSTRUMENTAL*) as the Combo begins to play.*

KAY It's a wobbly feeling.
I have a commercial feeling.
Be sexy in business.
Be successful at night ...
Let the children do the shopping!
Watch out for those loose ends!
Those flying tips ... Think of a color ...
Think of a number ... so stop.
And ask yourself ... "Well, why not?"

The UNIFORM PEOPLE *disappear as* PEOPLE *in* SPORTS GEAR *come out (waders, exercisers, hockey players, swimmers).*

KAY Now look at this ...
Now look over here ...
There is more than enough
to go around ... Watch out for
dimpling on the knees and elbows!
Now look at me ...
Relax in the video lounge,
it's a scientific lifestyle!
You are on the go ... Wear cool blue
to soothe those jangled nerves.
You're supercharged.

Service with Style

Effectively dressed employees are part of a "living decor" that sets a restaurant's tone. Carefully considered employee clothing also boosts the wearer's morale, perhaps leading to increased output. And their sharp appearance makes employees seem more competent to patrons.

Food Service Marketing Magazine

The 80s Lifestyle

A Midtown tennis court.
Windsurfing, jet skiing.
Park picnics,
Sundeck cocktails ...

The bright sun, cool water, blue skies to erase the fluorescent bulbs, conferences, phone calls.

Dorothée Bis Fashion

Off with Their Hats!

August 7, 1984 In a rare display of public pique, England's prim and prudish Queen Elizabeth flew into a tizzy over the wild and wacky hats worn by high society ladies ... at a posh Ascot racetrack.

Weekly World News

How to Be Plump *and* Pretty

April 24, 1984 Thousands of buxom lovelies around the country are tossing out diet books and daring to be plump and pretty—you can do the same ... Go with V-necks, scoopnecks, and square necks. Wear straight-legged pants and high boots.

Weekly World News

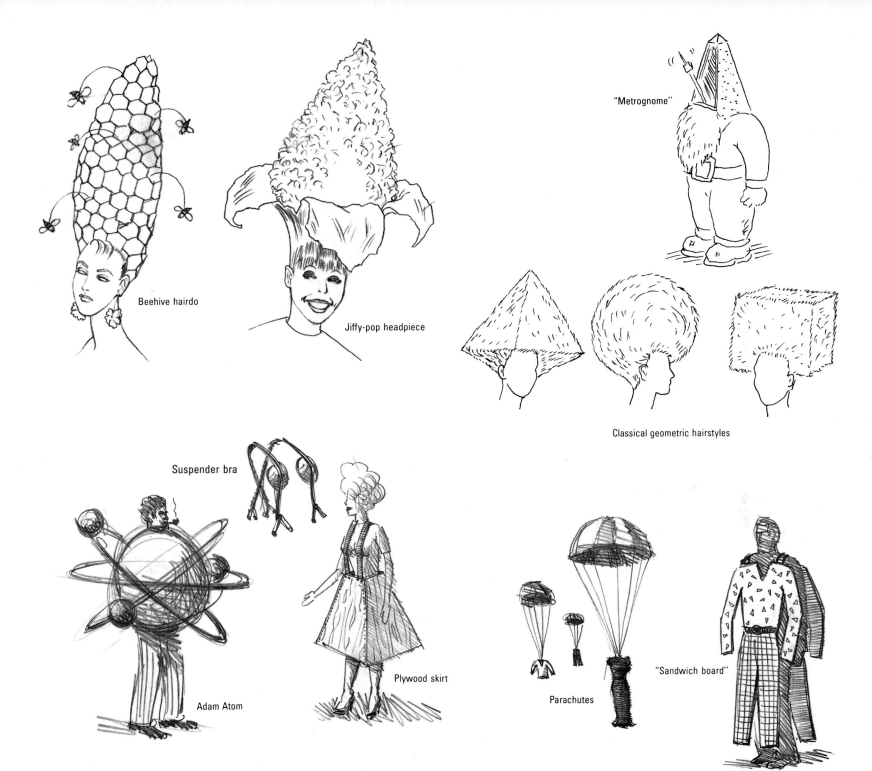

Beehive hairdo

Jiffy-pop headpiece

"Metrognome"

Classical geometric hairstyles

Suspender bra

Adam Atom

Plywood skirt

Parachutes

"Sandwich board"

Drawings by Nancy Reese and Phil Garner

You're gliding through the days ...
It's an action dream ...
It's a metallic evening ...
You are running through an airport ...
It's an exotic location ...
Get in tune with your surroundings ...
Sink in ... blend in ...
Get ahead and disappear ...

The SPORTS PEOPLE *leave and out come the* CHILDREN DRESSED AS ADULTS.

KAY   Think of where you'll be each day and coordinate your outfit to match. If the room is pink, you're in the pink! Your style says, "Don't count me out ... don't count on me." You have a right ... It's all you! ... There oughta be a law!

Kay begins to sing.

KAY   When you were little
You dreamed you were big
You must have been something
A real tiny kid

The CHILDREN *leave the stage and* BIG AND BEAUTIFUL PEOPLE *come out.*

KAY   You wish you were me
I wish I was you
Now don't you wake up
The dream will come true

CHORUS
Every dream has a name
And names tell your story
This song is your dream
You're the dream operator

The BIG AND BEAUTIFUL PEOPLE *disappear and out comes the* URBAN CAMOUFLAGE GROUP (*2 live grass suits, the fake grass family of 4, people dressed in foliage from each season, and last, people in clothes patterned after building materials ... wood, bricks, stone, and a Grecian column*).

BANANA LEAF
DRESS.

tulle
under.

Jackie
Kennedy
Boxwood
ensemble.

cherry or
holly
buttons

bird nest
bag

plastic
water
repellent

AUTUMN OAK LEAF
ensemble.

CAPE

STRETCH pants
w/ crewled
tree pattern.

Drawings by Adelle Lutz

ML

KAY It's bigger than life
      You know it's all me
      My face is a book
      But it's not what it seems

      Three angels above
      The whole human race
      They dream us to life
      They dream me a face

CHORUS
      And every dream tells it all
      And this dream is your story
      You dreamed me a heart
      You're the dream operator

BRIDGE
      Shake-it-up dream
      Hi-di-ho dream
      Fix-it-up dream
      Look at me dream
      I've been waiting so long
      Now I am your dream

The URBAN CAMOUFLAGE PEOPLE *leave the stage as the* BRIDAL FINALE GROUP *comes out (a woman with a white swan headdress, 2 children bearing a water urn, a woman in an outfit modeled after a wedding cake, the* CUTE WOMAN *in a heart headdress, the* BRIDE *with a huge floral headdress).*

The CAMERA *moves to the* LYING WOMAN, *who is sitting at a table with a* YOUNG GIRL *watching the show.*

LYING WOMAN I used to be a French model ... They begged and begged me to be in the style show but just between you and me I'm on a very top priority secret mission ... so I'm trying to keep a low profile. I'm here to pass some classified information on to Mr. Earl Culver that will literally change the face of this nation ... He doesn't know it yet, but we are cosmically linked by a blue computer chip that I stole off a spaceship.

Weekly World News

Your Pants Can Kill You!

Hiroto Watanabe was an impeccable dresser, a fashion-conscious freak who always wore the right duds until one fateful night—his clothes killed him . . .

"It is my opinion the man would be alive today if not for the tight clothes he was wearing," said a doctor.

"They cut off the flow of blood to a main coronary artery, causing a heart attack."

"He wore hip-hugging jeans and tight-fitting T-shirts. He was an extremely style-conscious man," said a friend.

He-men who want to look macho in tight pants and flashy belts can pay dearly for the pleasure, according to [another doctor].

"Perhaps Watanabe would be alive today if he had not dressed that way."

The Sun

Everything Under the Sun

June 5, 1984 Stereo coats are the latest sound in fashion. Chicago's Mibuco Investments has designed a man's coat which will serenade you in stereo, with music coming from speakers located on the right and left collars. Governments are getting into the act too, for the company will build a two-way radio coat so spies can keep warm and informed at the same time.

The Sun

Shoes That Protect Valuables

June 5, 1984 You can protect yourself—or at least your valuables—from purse snatchers, thanks to a remarkable new invention.

The brain child of Rebecca Fenton and her boyfriend Jerry Cole, this incredible little device can also make it more convenient for you to get hold of your keys in a hurry.

"Jerry was fed up with me always losing my keys when I go shopping," says Rebecca.

. . . So he took a knife and cut a shelf in the cork sole of Rebecca's clogs, and then he slid a cardboard matchbox inside to be used as a drawer.

The Star

The Way You Walk and Dress Can Make Your Legs Look Great

June 12, 1984 Make the most of "foot doodles."

Many of us bounce or shake our legs when we're seated.

Turn these "doodle" actions into exercises. With heels on floor, use the big toe to trace circles, stars, or your favorite doodle.

Remember the famous Lubbock lights? The most scientifically documented sightings of UFO's in the history of the world ... Well, I was politely minding my own business at a weenie roast right off of Levelland Highway when they zapped me up ... You wouldn't believe the stuff I know ... For instance—our dear Civic Leader just happens to be a walk-in from another planet. I believe it's Pluto—or maybe Venus ... He's real good lookin'.

KAY   Hard to forget
Hard to go on
When you fall asleep
You're out on your own

Let go of your life
Grab on to my hand
Here in the clouds
Where we'll understand

CHORUS
And you dreamed it all
And this is your story
Do you know who you are?
You're the dream operator

And you dreamed it all
And this is your story
Do you know who you are?
You're the dream operator

The CUTE WOMAN, *entranced by the beauty of it all, loses track of where she is. Her eyes begin to glaze over. She gently swoons and falls out of* FRAME.

She ends up on a table, passed out.

General commotion.

Fade up on: Exterior, Field—(Day)

A YOUNG COUPLE *walks away from the* CAMERA *on the flat landscape. They move slowly and hold each other's hands.*

MAN   You know, I don't think I've ever felt this way before.

WOMAN   I know, me neither.

Las Floristas Charity Ball, California

84

ML

MAN   My stomach feels all fluttery.

He makes a motion like his stomach is turning round and round.

WOMAN   It's great though ... huh?

He stops and turns and looks at her.

MAN   Yeah, I guess ... These people at work must think I'm going nuts though.

WOMAN   Well, if this is being nuts ... then I don't ever want to be sane.

He runs his hand through her hair. She puts her arms around him and they kiss. We see them now from a long way off ... two tiny figures merging against the vast landscape.

WOMAN (V.O.)   Ooh! ... Did you fart?

The CAMERA PANS *around to:*

Exterior, Stage Site (in the field)—(Twilight)

The last workers are packing up and driving off. By this time, the whole framework for the stage is up ... A construction of steel poles in the shape of a rectangular box ... with an opening in the front.

A temporary stage of wooden planks has been laid down while the construction continues. A few work lights are left on ... the whole scene has an eerie appearance as the sun goes down.

The NIGHT WATCHMAN *looks around, then slowly climbs up onto the stage. He takes a position at center stage and stares out into space. Suddenly, he throws his hands up into the air and begins to* SING *an aria from an opera.*

Cut to: Exterior, Mirrored Office Building—(Twilight)

An office building on the flat landscape. One light is still on in an office, allowing us to see into that room, while all the other windows are virtual mirrors, reflecting the landscape. As the CAMERA

moves in we see a MAN in this cubicle, moving around. He seems busy. He briefly looks out the window, almost right at us. As the CAMERA MOVES EVEN CLOSER we can see what he is really doing ... He is working out some wild dance steps and gazing at his reflection in the window, which is now a mirror on his side. The CAMERA MOVES CLOSER, he wiggles a leg ... rubs his tummy ... freezes ... points at his reflection ... brings his arm down and stylishly puts it in his pocket ... as he does a little shuffle. His movements are a little stiff, but quite sincere. He sticks out one leg ... tosses his foot around ... slowly swivels ... turns back to check himself in the mirror ... quickly stands up straight ... freezes for a moment, then quickly leans sideways, as far as he can go. Gaining courage, he executes a flashy spin and drop, ending in a dramatic freeze.

Cut to: Exterior, a Bar on the Highway—(Night)

A neon sign outside is flashing "Dining ... Dancing."

Interior, Bar—(Night)

LOUIS FYNE is on a date with the LYING WOMAN.

LYING WOMAN   Oh, I'm in the construction business. Got work going on at 5 sites right now. I bought a condo last week. Real close to here as a matter of fact. I think I might buy another one next week. Darlin', I just have a feel for it. You know what I mean? Course, being overly psychic hasn't hurt anything. Listen, Mr. Frye ...

LOUIS   Uh, Mr. Fyne. Louis.

LYING WOMAN   Well, Louis darlin' ... I'll tell you something if you promise not to tell another living soul ... Louis mimes, "locks," his mouth shut. But I believe that part of my extra psychic ability is connected up with my being born with a tail ... Honest to almighty God, I had a little hairy tail about an inch long ...

88

GC

It was surgically removed when I was just two years old. My mamma kept it in a fruit jar up in the medicine cabinet ... right between the 4-way cold tablets and the monkey blood ... For years I'd get up in the morning and first thing brush my teeth and stare at my own tail at the same time ... Something like that can give you power.

Louis looks around the room ... feeling surprised at being privy to such amazing information.

Then Mama got a wild hair one Sunday morning and decided to take it to a big old swap meet and make lots of money off of it ... So she sold it to Lyndon Johnson's top secret-service agent ... He told a good personal friend of mine that he was gonna sell it to the Smithsonian Institute. Might as well ... It wouldn't do him any good ... LOUIS LAUGHS *in agreement.* You know, Mr. Fyne, I could write a book, and it would be a best-seller.

LOUIS   I'm a writer too, sort of. I wrote a little song. I'm doing it for the show on Friday ... I'm a little nervous. Hope I can do it.

LYING WOMAN   Oh, songs are easy for me. I wrote Billy Jean *and* most of Elvis's songs.

LOUIS   Elvis?

LYING WOMAN   We worked out a deal. They pay me and I keep quiet. Somebody has to do it. Would you excuse me a minute, punkin'?

She gets up and leaves.

LOUIS   Sure, sure ... I'll be right here.

A WORKER *from Varicorp walks over to* LOUIS.

WORKER   Hey, Bear! How's it going?

LOUIS   It's going good ... good. Listen, I think this woman really likes me ... and she's done *every-thing* ... It's incredible! So don't hang around when she gets back, huh?

WORKER   That's cool ... Hey, what about the one you flew in?

Golfing Green Estates, Dallas

LOUIS   Oh, man! . . . I had a picture of her face, right? . . . And that matched up O.K. . . . But her body was huge! She looked like a refrigerator with a head. I don't know, next time I'll insist on full body shots . . . know what I mean?

Woah! . . . here she comes . . . see you later, huh?

Cut to: Exterior, Upper-Middle-Class Suburban Home: The Culvers'—(Night)

A New England–style house in Texas.

VOICE OF KAY CULVER   Shall we take a moment to give thanks?

Interior, Dining Room—(Night)

The Civic Leader, EARL, *and his wife,* KAY. *A fairly well-to-do family. The son (*LARRY*) is about 13, and the daughter (*LINDA*) is a little older. The* NARRATOR *is joining them as they sit down to dinner.*

KAY   Amen.

(They all raise their heads and unfold their napkins.)

NARRATOR   This looks wonderful, Mrs. Culver.

KAY   Thank you.

EARL   Oh, look . . . Pigs in a blanket.

KAY   Linda, will you ask your father to pass this to our guest?

(They pass the plate along.)

CIVIC LEADER   Linda, will you ask your mother to pass the mustard?

LINDA   Mom, Dad wants some mustard.

She passes it over. The table is arranged with one main course, a lobster, which is surrounded by vegetables, some plates of condiments and various side dishes on a nearby lazy susan.

LJ

Weekly World News

Loving Couple Hasn't Spoken for 31 Years!

March 13, 1984 The Rolfes, who married in 1949, have lived under the same roof, slept in the same bed and raised two normal, well-adjusted children, all without uttering a single word between them since 1953 . . .

"Incredibly, this lifelong silent treatment began with a silly misunderstanding, [said their 34-year-old son, David.] "My father is a respected attorney and my mother is a biology teacher. They had been married four years when she accused him of having an affair with his secretary. Well, there was no affair. Dad's secretary was nearly 80.

"They had a big argument in which Dad called Mom a jealous fool. She said that if she was jealous, it was only because she loved him and that she wouldn't speak to him again until he apologized for calling her a fool. Dad said he would apologize when pigs fly."

Those were the last words the couple said to each other. "My sister and I grew up thinking it was normal for parents not to talk to each other. At dinner Dad would say, 'Tell your mother the pot roast is excellent.' Or Mom would say, 'Ask your father if he would like more tea.'

"When I was 16 we were all shopping downtown. Mom stepped out in front of a bus. Dad saw it coming and shouted at me to shout at Mom to get out of the way."

David said that [after] he and his sister [had grown] up, his parents hired a live-in maid so they wouldn't have to talk to each other.

Rolfe, 60, said, "I haven't spoken to Peggy in 31 years and maybe that's why our marriage has lasted."

"He's a stubborn man," [said Mrs. Rolfe,] "but I still love him and you can tell him that for me."

ML

CIVIC LEADER   Linda, will you ask your mom how the Fashion Show went today?

LINDA   Sure, Dad ... *(turns to her mother)* ... Mom, how'd it go today? ...

KAY   Well, Linda, you tell him it was just wonderful ... although one woman did have an accident, but it wasn't serious. He should have been there ... he would have been proud of me.

The NARRATOR *is a little puzzled by this rather odd behavior, but as the Culvers seem to treat it as normal, he decides to ignore it for the time being.*

LINDA   Mom says it went great, Dad. Says you shoulda been there. You woulda been proud of her.

NARRATOR   I was quite impressed, Mrs. Culver. I don't usually go to that kind of thing, but this was really something ... Do you do this every year?

LARRY   Nah, this is just for the sesquicentennial.

NARRATOR   Oh, yeah?

LARRY   You gonna film all the stuff day after tomorrow?

Larry reaches over as he talks and spins a large lazy susan in the middle of the table ...

NARRATOR   I hope so ... it depends on whether your dad says it's O.K. Are you gonna be in the parade?

LARRY   Anderson Auto is lending us a red convertible for the parade!

KAY   Would you like some gherkins? Linda, ask your dad if he wants some.

A glamorous CLOSE-UP *of the food on the plate. It's been carefully arranged to create a curious abstract design.*

LINDA   Hey, Dad, want some gherkins? They're good for ya.

CIVIC LEADER   Just put them in the center, please. *(to the Narrator)* Larry might have a future at Varicorp. With his young discipline and systems consciousness, he'll go a long way ... They're growing like there's no tomorrow.

LARRY Yeah, well, Bob says that Amalgamated Data over in Richardson just went under. That's no tomorrow, all right.

NARRATOR Yes, I heard about that too . . . *(to the Civic Leader)* Mr. Culver, do you ever wonder that Virgil is becoming too reliant on one industry, like Varicorp? Becoming a one-company town?

Very QUIET MUSIC *begins in the background . . . soft and gentle.*

CIVIC LEADER *(changes his tone of voice)* Yes, that can happen . . . sometimes people tend to lose their heads when they hear the magical word "high-tech." Lemme show you what I think is happening.

LINDA Do you hear music?

No one answers.

The Civic Leader points to groups of foods on the lazy susan near the center of the table. His tone has now changed to that of a public speaker.

CIVIC LEADER Mainframe . . .

His hand hovers over another group on the lazy susan.

CIVIC LEADER Microprocessor . . .

He moves over to another group. It's like a religious intonation.

CIVIC LEADER Semiconductor . . .

LINDA AND LARRY *(encouraging him)* Go for it, Daddy!

CIVIC LEADER If this is the town . . .

He points to the main course, surrounded by decorative vegetables. It seems to "light up" as he gestures to it.

CIVIC LEADER And here is the workplace . . . *He gestures to the lazy susan with its asparagus. It lights up also.* And here are the goods and their distribution network.

He removes some of the asparagus and makes a "road" across the table. Linda and Larry help.

96

LJ

CIVIC LEADER Most middle-class people have worked for these large corporations ... like Varicorp here ... or for the government itself. (*He gestures to the main dish.*)

CIVIC LEADER Now, for middle-class people, the rewards for individual effort have been pretty slim ...

He picks up the container of peppers from the lazy susan. They also light up. He begins to dish out minuscule portions of peppers to the family and narrator.

CIVIC LEADER ... First, the government takes its slice ...

He gives part of his own peppers to the main-course dish.

CIVIC LEADER ... or there's no reward at all ... like in some Communist countries.

Larry is not given any peppers at all.

But now that's starting to change. Some of the scientists and engineers are moving off from their employers, like Varicorp, and are starting new companies, marketing their own inventions.

He moves the small red and yellow tomatoes that surround the asparagus dish off the lazy susan, and moves them to the far edges of the table along the asparagus "road."

NARRATOR Excuse me, Mr. Culver, I forgot what these peppers represent.

We see the table from above.

CIVIC LEADER Ah hah! ... it all spins back to the middle, see ...

The central lazy susan begins to turn ... slowly.

Here we are right now ... (*He points to the main course.*) Our way of doing business is based on the past. We should try to keep these guys in Virgil ...

He moves the mini-red and yellow tomatoes at the edges back around the lobster ... forming a ring around it.

... even though they leave Varicorp.

The kids join in, adding items to the cluster in the middle. From overhead, a pattern or diagram is emerging.

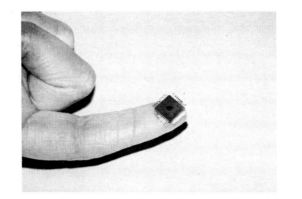

Texas Monthly

Behind the Lines
by Gregory Curtis

June 1984 Once everyone believed in work. If you worked hard, you would get rich. Later on you would get to go to heaven too. This seductively appealing doctrine—you get paid now and you get paid later—was known as the work ethic ...

Does anyone still believe in the old work ethic?

No, not really.

What happened?

The religious part went first ... Next, with the coming of general prosperity, the belief in thrift atrophied. The government discouraged saving by taxing earnings and encouraged borrowing by exempting from taxes the interest and sometimes, depending on what was bought and why, the principal. Meanwhile, inflation destroyed the economic benefit of saving. The result is that today America is so oriented toward consumption that a return to thriftiness would strangle our economy. And last, the sort of rugged, individual, hard work the ethic demanded disappeared into bureaucracies, never to be heard from again ... Today the American middle class is far more likely to work for some large organization like a corporation or a government agency where the rewards for individual effort are slim. But now even that's started to change ...

There is a large group who follow the new work ethic and are working harder than people used to work. But the new believers are not working in order to earn a place in heaven, nor are they working to pay off the mortgage and put the kids through college, the way people did in the fifties.

The believer in the new work ethic is a maverick, working for himself and answerable only to himself. The rejection of authority and the yearning for individuality that blossomed in the sixties have finally invaded the business world ... New believers want to make money so they can indulge their own idea of personal growth ... Everything is a part of one life. The believer wants to exceed his personal bottom line.

Can you recognize a person who follows the new work ethic when you see one?

Yes, you can. He's dressed casually and never wears a tie. He works for himself or for a small, new company where he has a lot of freedom. He works his own hours ... His business and personal philosophy—always one and the same—is high risk, high reward ... He believes in "wellness," and despite a demanding schedule, he exercises, watches his diet, and takes it easy with booze and dope ...

The founder of a small computer company or an independent software writer is the quintessential believer in the new work ethic.

Texas Monthly

Broke in the Promised Land

by Peter Applebome

July 1982 Odessa is usually thought of as the one place where there's always work, the most robust of the oil field boom towns. But with the downturn in the oil industry, even Odessa is feeling the pinch . . .

"All the people who've been discarded from all over the universe are coming here," says one man who has lived in Odessa for a number of years. "It's a free country and they're permitted to migrate where they want, but dammit, I wish they'd go somewhere else. I feel like we're living in some sort of invasion."

. . . "Louisiana, Michigan, Mississippi, Georgia, North Carolina. You name the fifty states, we've got 'em here," [says a county sheriff.] "You look at some of these people, they're filthy, with no shirts, and they have bumper stickers saying things like 'Happiness is a good screw.' They might be the finest Christian people in the world, but until you got to know them, you wouldn't expect it."

"A year ago they were begging people to come to this town," [said an unemployed worker.] "Now the chamber of commerce wants to get rid of them."

"A lot of people have come in and made a lot of money and are well off today, and when they moved in here they didn't have anything either," [says an attorney.] "They found their rainbow here, and I'd hate to see that change."

Inc. Magazine

The Second Industrial Revolution

An economist and a political scientist find that changing tastes and new technology may be ushering in an age of craftsmanship.

by Karl Frieden

September 1985 The first industrial divide ushered in the reign of mass production, with rigidly defined divisions of labor, standardized products, and large-scale corporations. The new developments portend a shift toward an economy of "flexible specialization," with less hierarchical organizations, more (and more customized) consumer goods, and increased market share for smaller-scale companies.

The bad news is that the economic turbulence of the past decade is neither temporary nor an aberration. Mass-production society is under siege from forces that are so powerful that the halcyon days of the postwar period have been banished forever. The good news is that out of this constant turmoil may emerge a less rigidified economy: efficient, yet on a human scale, and flexible enough to avoid the extremes of the business cycle . . .

Michael Piore: What is involved is a change in the role of small and medium-sized companies. We're moving toward a situation where the small company is the dynamic leading edge of the economy . . . We dispute the notion that mass production is the one and only path of technical progress. Mass production, with its lower costs per unit of production, supplanted craft production during the first industrial divide in the nineteenth century. But the historical circumstances have changed. New technologies, like the computer, have developed, which have lowered the cost and increased the innovative capabilities of craft production. So you're getting a more dynamic craft system—what we call flexible specialization.

Charles Sabel: Mass production involves single-purpose machines that are built to make that commodity, and only that commodity . . .

Craft production is the reverse. Skilled workers use general-purpose machinery to turn out a wide and constantly changing assortment of goods for shifting markets . . .

You can think of it almost like a musical instrument. If you have a musical instrument, then you can have a thousand different people play anything, anytime at all, on it. Whereas in mass production, it's much more like a record; you can just play it . . . The opportunities are much greater today for small, dynamic companies . . .

The industrial world is saturated with the classic goods of mass production . . . This has brought the major industrial economies into direct competition for one another's markets and for those of the developing world . . .

Piore: In the 1950s, there was an enormous amount of consumerism that was based on having the mass product, and everybody wanting the same thing. Now people want to be unique or different . . . And the cost of indulging individuality has fallen enormously.

Sabel: The personal computer or the videocassette recorder are very easily customized to suit individual taste. The actual hardware cost is going to zero. All the money is being spent on adding things to it and making it into the thing you want.

Piore: Smaller-scale companies are becoming less dependent on large companies; they are engaging in more cooperative and interactive relationships with larger companies.

Inc.: So mass production—huge quantities of standardized goods—limits the imagination as well as the marketplace?

Piore: Right.

Texas Monthly

Death of a Computer

by Joseph Nocera

April 1984 . . . Texas Instruments, the company that had put more computers into American homes than anyone else, was pulling out of the home computer business . . . Who could have imagined that it would end this way?

Just before Christmas in 1982, one of the men in charge of producing the TI home computer had to have emergency surgery, and as he was being wheeled into the operating room, the doctor walking beside him found out where he worked. "Do you have anything to do with the ninety-nine four A?" asked the doctor. "Yes," the man replied. "I've been looking for that computer everywhere," said the doctor. "Do you think you could get me one?" When they got into the operating room, the doctor told the anesthesiologist that the patient worked for TI and could get a 99/4A—and the anesthesiologist asked for one too. Right there in the operating room!

. . . TI quickly asserted its superiority in the marketplace with a four-bit chip called the TMS 1000. [It] soon became the most ubiquitous chip in the business, used in video games, calculators, microwave ovens, and hundreds of other electronic products . . .

. . . But did Everyman need—or even want—a computer in his home? Was a home computer an appliance or was it a toy? Was it the beginning of the electronic future or was it the hula hoop of the eighties? TI thought the machine would sell. Convincing people that they needed it could come later.

CIVIC LEADER   See, their rejection of authority has invaded the business world. *He shakes the main course at the tower of asparagus (the workplace). For the time being it's creating confusion and chaos.*

Earl takes a food item, holds it over the "Town" (the main course) and crushes it ... it plops or crumbles all over the dish. The children make dams and volcanoes out of the food on their own plates.

CIVIC LEADER   They don't work for money anymore ... or to earn a place in heaven ... which was a big motivating factor once, believe you me.

He holds up a cluster of asparagus ... and "hovers" or "makes it float" above the table. Then he tosses it up, and it falls everywhere.

CIVIC LEADER   Economics has become a spiritual thing.

Earl makes an expansive gesture. Various items on the table seem to glow ... the lighting has slowly become more "glamorous."

CIVIC LEADER   They're working and inventing because they like it! It's a whole new philosophy ...

He refers to the "Scientist & Engineer" foodstuffs which are now in a very organized arrangement around the main course. It looks like a mandala or concentric circles.

CIVIC LEADER   I must admit, it frightens me a little bit. They don't see any difference between working ... *Earl takes two circular fish cakes, and works them like gears. ...* and not working.

Close-ups of the children's plates ... they have built things out of their food.

CIVIC LEADER   Everything is a part of one's life ... Linda ... Larry ... there's no concept of weekends anymore!

Various close-ups as music builds ... from overhead we can see that Earl has turned the table into a giant diagram of the patterns of economic growth and change in his community.

Fade to black on everything but the food-dish lights.

Food Styling

Food styling is an art form but it's one of the most decadent art forms around. You need to be able to appreciate something totally absurd to enjoy and appreciate the art of food styling. Did you know that when you see ice cream in a commercial it's probably not ice cream but whipped potatoes because ice cream would melt under the movie lights? Sometimes they put rocks in the soup to make it look chunkier. Do you like parsley? I really like parsley, but when I'm eating parsley I kind of feel like I'm eating the design and not really eating the food.

Food styling for restaurants or at home dinners is an art form that you place before you, appreciate for a minute, and eat. It never has time to get stale. You never have time to get tired of looking at it or to worry about whether this should be here or over there, or whether it was done right. You only have time to enjoy it and then consume it. If only a lot of art hanging on a lot of walls was like that.

ML

Exterior, Computer Guy's Home—(Dawn) The sun rising over the flat landscape . . . A few houses can be seen scattered here and there. A slightly rundown rural house trailer is surrounded by loads of junked electrical equipment. There is a satellite dish and an antenna outside.

Interior, Computer Guy's Home—(Morning)

The equipment consists of a variety of high-tech junk scrounged from various sources over the years. It surrounds the whole room and reaches almost to the ceiling in many places. In the foreground we see a work table/desk with a computer terminal on it. Behind this, in the middle of the room, is a kind of sunken area, or pit, which contains a rather ominous-looking piece of large equipment. Lots of BUZZING *and* CRACKLING SOUNDS. *The Computer Guy is showing Mr. Tucker around.*

COMPUTER GUY   I got that piece from the power company. A real beauty, mmm? You know, if Miss Rollings wanted to, she could get a computer and be real organized.

Mr. Tucker looks around with curiosity . . . he picks up a piece of equipment.

COMPUTER GUY   I broadcast only the best music . . . I'm really into music.

MR. TUCKER   Does this make music? *(looking at the piece of equipment)*

COMPUTER GUY   Nah . . . Nah . . . the tapes and records are over here . . . I invented this idea that music is like words . . . or pictures . . . and anybody can understand them . . . so for the people that *must* be out there . . . *(he looks up toward the heavens)* . . . music is the best . . . check it out . . .

He puts on a tape or record and adjusts a few dials and switches. Out comes some ethereal "New Age" music.

COMPUTER GUY   *This* is what I call universal music . . . I wish someone was playing something like this on Friday . . . can you imagine all that energy beaming out?

Freedom of Information

The electronic cottage: it really is coming true. Look at all the apartments or mobile homes with modems, computers, and satellite dishes. People are putting themselves in touch with anything they want, anywhere in the world. We can receive information about anything, anytime, anywhere. And with a little creativity, we can tap into anything. They can delay our access, but it's pretty difficult to put a lock and key on what's in the airwaves. It becomes harder and harder to prohibit the free flow of information, whether it's television signals or computer data. People can tape records, or Xerox pages of a book. This free information flow changes the whole value system from one that emphasizes the information itself to one that emphasizes how the stuff is organized and how it's used.

Life itself is a self-perpetuating organization of a particular kind. When we think of life from outer space, we tend to think it will look like us—at least that it will have a humanoid shape. It doesn't have to. It could be in the form of a gaseous cloud. Life forms like these couldn't even land in a flying saucer. Carl Jung wrote a book on flying saucers. He says people who believe in saucers are bringing religion up to date, making it high-tech.

Golfing Green Estates, Dallas

LJ

MR. TUCKER   I don't know too much about the *outer space* ...

A computer printer bursts into life. The screen lights up and the printer STARTS CLICKING *away.*

COMPUTER GUY   You know, these machines talk to themselves. I've had some weird shit left on here in the middle of the night.

MR. TUCKER   It's always the middle of the night somewhere. The same thing happens at my house.

The Computer Guy flips some switches and the large device in the pit begins to HUM.

COMPUTER GUY   You got computers at your place? Well, I guess just about everybody does now. *(looks at the thing in the pit)* Good night for it.

He hands Mr. Tucker the repaired TV *remote switch.*

COMPUTER GUY   Tell Miss Rollings thanks for the set ... it's got stuff they just don't make anymore.

Mr. Tucker looks at a bank of funky black-and-white monitors ... Most of the images on them seem to be flat, empty fields.

MR. TUCKER   That's a beautiful picture.

Mr. Tucker begins to head for the door as the Computer Guy raps.

COMPUTER GUY   Well, it could be a lot sharper ... you know, the government has all the *really* good stuff ... But, you know what I think? ... I think there's an organization above that! ... They have stuff even the government doesn't know about.

Yeah, there's something out there all right. I know *you* feel it ... There's a plan of some kind ... People are being prepared ... people are being affected ...

John Shepard

Life Beyond Earth

by Douglas Curran

Summer 1984 John Shepherd is trying to contact extraterrestrial life. For years now, each morning at ten he begins broadcasting music and binary signals from Earth Station Radio . . .

"The point of this is to broadcast the human species—the energy within, as a being, a creative entity. It's important to express that, not just to put anything out there."

John's station has been in operation for nearly eleven years. In a black pit are sunk large hydro transformers scrounged from the local power utility. Rising out of this well is the accelerator tower. Plates and grids bracketed with insulators set up a fierce buzzing as the signal charge crosses over them in a fan of blue arcs into the antennae. The saturated magnetic field ionizes the air, leaving the smell of ozone.

Overhead hang service boards and modules mounted with UV meters, phase loop converters, signal strength indicators, manometers, voltmeters, pulse shapers, pulse shape monitors, potentiometers, switches, patch cords, ICs, LEDs, and ready lights. All of it alive and talking to someone or something, immeasurable miles away. Coupled with the signaling gear is a system for detecting UFOs, in operation twenty-four hours a day.

John and his grandma live frugally; they do without natural gas service in order to funnel money into materials for the project. Grandpa Lamb used to grumble about the growing incursion of equipment and paraphernalia into the living room. Eventually, Mr. and Mrs. Lamb were left with only a small settee scrunched into a corner between whole walls taken up by John's consoles and oscilloscopes.

Grandpa Lamb died two years ago. Now John and his grandmother make a good team. Together they built an addition on the house for John's burgeoning equipment and put a rocking chair in the living room for Mrs. Lamb.

The air smells of transistors. It's peaceful and reassuring. Often John will go in there by himself and sit late into the night, looking at the lights and listening to the transformers hum.

The Night of the Hackers

by Richard Sandza

November 12, 1984 Computer bulletin boards are hangouts of a new generation of vandals. These precocious teen-agers use their electronic skills to play hide-and-seek with computer and telephone security forces . . .

Hook up and you see a broad choice of topics offered. For Phone Phreaks, Phreakenstein's Lair is a potpourri of phone numbers, access codes and technical information. For computer hackers—who dial into other people's computers—Ranger's Lodge is chock-full of phone numbers and passwords for government, university and corporate computers . . .

You have your computer dial the Yale computer. Bingo—the words Yale University appear on your screen. You enter a password. A menu appears. You hang up in a sweat. You are now a hacker . . .

Do you have any ties to or connections with any law enforcement agency or any agency which would inform such a law enforcement agency of this bulletin board?

Such is the welcoming message from Plovernet, a Florida board known for its great hacker/phreak files . . .

Each board has different commands. So far you haven't had the nerve to type "C," which summons the system operator for a live, computer-to-computer conversation. The time, however, has come to ask a few questions of the "sysop."

Hello . . . What kind of computer do you have?

Contact. The sysop is here. You get "talking" . . . Finally, he asks: "How old are you?" "How old are YOU?" you reply. "15," he types. Once he knows you're old enough to be his father . . . the chat continues, "What time is it there?" "Just past midnight," you reply. Expletive. "It's 3:08," sysop types. "I must be going to sleep. I've got school tomorrow." The cursor dances. "Thank You for Calling." The screen goes blank.

Bummed to the Minimum, Hacked to the Max

by Stephen Levy

In 1959 the M.I.T. Tech Model Railroad club discovered the TX-0 . . .

Computing with the TX-0 was like playing a musical instrument upon which you could improvise, compose and wail like a banshee with total creative abandon . . .

The hackers began to think that by devoting their technical abilities to computing, with a devotion rarely seen outside of monasteries, they were becoming the vanguard of a daring symbiosis between man and machine . . . Their tiny society, on intimate terms with the TX-0, had been piecing together a body of a concepts and mores. **The Hacker Ethic: Access to computers—and anything which might teach you something about the way the world works—should be unlimited and total.**

They believed that essential lessons could be learned about systems—about the world—by taking things apart, seeing how they work and using this knowledge to create new and even more interesting things . . . **All information should be free** . . . particularly when the information was in the form of a computer program . . . Instead of having to write your own version of the same program, the best version would be available to everyone.

But there was at least one hacker who was far from delighted at this demonstration of sharing and cooperation—Bill Gates. He and his partner had sold their BASIC [program language] to MITS on the basis that they would earn royalties for every copy sold . . .

All hell broke loose in the hacker community. As the number of computers in use grew, a good piece of software became something which could make a lot of money—if hackers did not consider it well within their provinces to pirate the software. No one seemed to object to a software author getting something for his work—but neither did the hackers want to let go of the idea that computer programs belonged to everybody.

Cut to: Exterior, Fellowship Hall—(Day)

A boxy building on the flat landscape ... probably prefab metal structure. A number of cars are parked outside.

Interior, Fellowship Hall—(Day)

There is a podium front and center ... a "PREACHER" addresses the CONGREGATION. Behind him sits a CHOIR and to his left are a number of MUSICIANS, among them RAMON, who is seated at a keyboard instrument.

The Speaker is dressed in a conservative suit, capped by an enormous shock of pure white hair.

PREACHER   It thrills me! It thrills me! We can build a nation inside a nation right where we are! The choice is yours. I'm not a joiner. I'm not a member of the John Birch Society or the Communist Party.

We see LOUIS FYNE in the audience. In another section we see EARL, the Civic Leader, and his wife, KAY.

PREACHER   Let's look at what's happened to the national morals since WW II.

The Preacher motions to a screen which has been set up above the choir.

PREACHER   We lost the Vietnam war ...

An IMAGE of LBJ appears on the screen ... and is replaced by one of NIXON.

PREACHER   The movies and television are filled with characters I don't even wanna know! Not in this life!

On another corner of the screen appear images of JOAN COLLINS ... JR ... MR. T ... the guys from CHIP's ... and an MTV V.J.

PREACHER   The farmer is in trouble. The small businessman is in trouble!

IMAGES of abandoned storefronts and broken-down farm buildings ... a farmer placing a "for sale" sign on his property ... RAMON hits a BLAST on the keyboard as punctuation.

Victorious Life Fellowship, Hewlett, Texas

DB

PREACHER   Unemployment is skyrocketing ... Texas is STILL paying for John Kennedy's death, my friends.

The LYING WOMAN *jumps up in her seat to testify.*

LYING WOMAN   It was *love* that killed John Kennedy! He should never have messed with me. ... Oh no! ...

As if in court, she raises her hand.

I know nothing, Your Honor. They wanted me to speak on 60 Minutes. Mike Wallace wants my body! I don't tell a soul ... they gave me so much money. What could I do?

PREACHER   *(a little surprised, but he continues)* Thank you. That's exactly what I'm talking about. Let's look at who's been running the country since WW II.

RAMON *builds up in volume on the keyboard and begins a series of* PUNCTUATIONS *and* BLASTS *of* SOUND. *At each climax, another* IMAGE *or* SYMBOL *appears on the screen: various public figures, politicians and industrialists interspersed with common items and symbols of contemporary life. A telephone ... an oil well ... scales of justice ... a book ... a dollar bill ... an airplane ... a radio ... a television ... a newspaper ... a stylized man, woman and child.*

PREACHER   *(points to the screen)* And *they* have some involvement in all of these ... What is the link? What do cars have to do with books? you might ask.

Various lines appear on the screen connecting the various symbols in a complicated web. The face of DAVID ROCKEFELLER *appears in the middle.*

PREACHER   The Trilateral Commission and The Council on Foreign Relations. Ever hear of them? Well, neither did I until I noticed the Chain of Coincidence.

We see a series of still photos of famous news events on the screen ...

ML

A series of dates appears on the screen . . . March 7, 1958 . . . July 16, 1962 . . . April 1977.

The news photos reappear in the shape of a world map.

The "Congregation" APPLAUDS *. . . Ramon runs up and down the keyboard. Someone* SHOUTS *out.*

PREACHER   They *know* what Bobby Ray Inman was
doing before he was running the microelectronics
and computer tech corporation? . . . Well, *guess!*

A photo of a DOOR *labeled* "AUTHORIZED
PERSONNEL ONLY" *. . . An image of a pyra-
mid with the eye on top superimposed on the door
. . . Ramon plays an* OMINOUS THEME.

PREACHER   A CIA Director . . . It's public knowledge!
Do you run out of Kleenex, paper towels, and
toilet paper at the same time? *You know it's true!*

*The level of excitement in the "Congregation" is
building. A* MAN SHOUTS *out:*

VOICE   IT'S ALL TRUE! . . .

PREACHER   Do you remember how Governor White
campaigned to get the MCC here?

*Ramon's keyboard playing begins to take on a
rhythm . . . a driving, insistent pulse that slowly
begins to build.*

PREACHER   Do you know what their goal is? Elvis did!

On the screen a photo of ELVIS *shaking hands
with* NIXON.

A YOUNG MAN *raises his hand as if to answer the
question.*

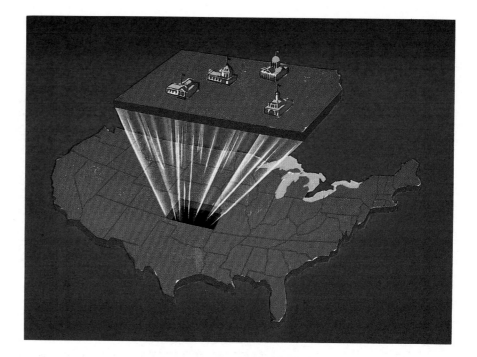

**Conspiracies Unlimited
A Journal of Research and Criticism**

The Gemstone File

Aristotle Onassis was secretly in
control of the United States for many
years, and along with the Mafia and
Rockefeller he was responsible for
the murders of Howard Hughes,
John F. Kennedy, Bobby Kennedy,
and Lyndon Johnson.

1957: Onassis is worried about the
growing power of Howard Hughes,
who is buying up politicians like
Richard Nixon. Onassis kidnaps
Hughes, shoots him full of heroin,
and takes him to a tiny Greek island
where he spends the rest of his life
in a vegetable state.

1959: Joseph Kennedy reminds
Onassis that the Greek owes him a
favor, so the Presidency is promised
to JFK. However, when Joe dies, the
Kennedy boys go off on their own
and start to offend the Mafia involv-
ing Jimmy Hoffa, opium, Cuba,
Hughes stock, etc.

1968: Bobby is killed by Onassis
gunmen, and Evelle Younger in California covers it up. Teddy feared for
his life, and went to Onassis to
swear eternal obedience. Jackie
was now "free" to marry Onassis,
who figured that since JFK has
welched on him he ought to have
Kennedy's gun and his girl. Mary Jo
Kopechne found out about all of this
and she had to be disposed of.

Salem Kirban On Major Cults

Jehovah's Witnesses

Why did Mrs. Russell ask for a divorce? Why did Judge Rutherford go to jail? Why is the date 1914 so important to them?

Mormonism

What strange findings that first began with eight barges and an ocean trip gave birth to an unusual cult? Why did they build a $2 million vault in the Granite Mountains near Salt Lake City? What state in the United States will possess the "keys to the world power"?

Christian Science

Why did Dr. Noyes remove Mary Baker Eddy's husband's heart and show it to her in her own living room?

News from the Posse Comitatus Sect

The people in control already are secretly using laser beams to "implant" invisible identification numbers on the foreheads of all infants born in hospitals. Only computers can see them [said a member of the Posse Comitatus sect].

The brains of aborted fetuses are used to make computer discs. "That's what computers run on."

Sermon by Identity Christian Minister

"There is a group of people, an elite, that's in control. The poor Jew that isn't in the elite, he gets exploited the same as everybody else. He's controlled, too; they exploit him so they can keep the Jews together as a whole. This elite that's always been in charge, they're the international bankers, the Bilderbergers, the CFR, the Fabians, the Illuminati. That's where the seat of the satanic

order is. Most of the people in our government are Fabians. Communism was built by this same group of people . . . The United Nations is the framework of the whole thing."

The World Power Foundation: Its Goals and Platform

The Foundation is aimed pretty frankly at the rich and would-be powerful; it translates their desire for slaves and control into a workable, systematic social policy.
• *Excitement is more important than equality;*
• *Might and right are not exactly the same, but after a few years no one will know the difference;*
• *Most people are actually looking to give up their freedom, provided they can find the right idol; you should be looking for ways they can serve you;*
• *Ultimately everything is food.*

Current Events
and Bible Prophecy Newsletter

Update The "666" System . . .
(The One World Government System)

March–April 1981 Tangible evidence is surfacing all over the world that the One World Government System prophesied by John 1900 years ago is emerging . . . I call it the "666 System." It will be fully implemented by the soon to be revealed Super World Dictator, the False Messiah, Mr. "666," the Antichrist . . .

The Universal Product Codemark is indeed becoming universal. Unless manufacturers resort to the

usage of these marks, their products cannot be checked out at the scanner check outs . . . "no man might . . . sell except that he had the mark" on his products. While the Social Security and IRS deny the reports of having mailed some checks with endorsements which require a mark on forehead or hand, my sources indicate a machine has already been designed for that express purpose . . . the Electronic Fund Transfer System will be seized by the next Super World Dictator, who will "cause all to receive a mark." . . .

Soon you will receive a Final Card and a Final Number. It will be as mandatory in distributing your earnings as the Social Security Card is now in earning your wages. It will be the Card by which you both *earn* and *distribute* your income . . .

Texas Monthly

A Call to Farms

When a populist orator warns of a conspiracy to take over the world, people in the farm belt listen.

by Nicholas Lemann

December 1978 The farmers of Panhandle, Texas, and their wives gathered at Panhandle High School . . . The man they had all come to hear was a farmer/orator . . .

"I love my God. I love my country. I love my family. Those are the three institutions that made this country great. And if you wanted to destroy this country, you'd destroy our faith in God, in the family, and in our country" [the farmer said].

He took a portentous sip of water. "Now let's talk about the Trilateral Commission."

The orator painstakingly laid out evidence of a massive worldwide conspiracy of businessmen, politicians, bankers, and academicians,

its goal the destruction of this country and its way of life, its nerve center, the Trilateral Commission . . . Founded by David Rockefeller in 1973 to foster cooperation between North America, Western Europe, and Japan, [it] had about 250 members, most of them the heads of huge corporations . . .

Carter appointed eighteen members of the Trilateral Commission to high positions in his government, including the vice presidency and the secretaryships of State, Defense, and Treasury . . .

The farmer sketched out the extent of Trilateral Commission control over the economy, the media, and education—they control, he said, either directly or indirectly, IBM, Kodak, the Chase Manhattan Bank, Exxon, Mobil, General Electric, the Bank of America, Equitable Life, the Ford Foundation, the Carnegie Foundation, ITT, American Motors, Safeway, Time Inc., NBC, CBS, the *New York Times*, the *Washington Post*, Pillsbury, General Foods, Coca-Cola, and many, many more . . .

"Everything led back [to the Trilateral Commission]" said another farmer and his wife from Panhandle, Texas, "and even farther back."

. . . The left's opinion was that the commission was plotting world fascism, the right's that it was plotting socialism, but their positions were otherwise identical . . .

If you are the paving contractor who has just moved to town, and the mayor always seems to give the street-patching contracts to the fellow who's in the Rotary Club, perhaps you'd start thinking, I bet they just give out those damn contracts *at* the Rotary Club meeting. If your life is controlled by forces you can't see or influence, it's a small step to begin thinking those forces are operating in other than completely random fashion.

PREACHER Artificial Intelligence! Robots! They'd like that, wouldn't they?

The SYMBOLS *of various large* CORPORATIONS *begin to appear on the screen in various sections.*

The corporate symbols combined with arcane RELIGIOUS *and* OCCULT SYMBOLS *and* ICONS *...a five-pointed star...a man with a pointed hat ...* DAVID STOCKMAN ... MR. T *and* NANCY REAGAN.

PREACHER SLEEP! ... SLEEP! ... One and one does not equal two! ... No sir! No sir!

His speaking becomes more CHANTLIKE *as he begins to* SWAY *to the tempo of the music ... A* DRUMMER *has now joined Ramon's keyboard.*

PREACHER Silicon Gulch! ... Silicon Prairie! Silicon Hill! ... Silicon Valley!

The LIGHTS *begin to* DIM *as the excitement rises.*

PREACHER Let us celebrate! You'd better wake up. It's late! It's late! It's late!

There is a discernible melody in the Preacher's CHANTING *now ... It has seamlessly evolved into a* SONG *... in* GOSPEL STYLE *... as he establishes the tune and structure the Choir soon joins in, answering his declamations and* SINGING *together in choruses.*

You got the CBS ... !
And the ABC ... !
You got *Time* and *Newsweek*!
Well, they're the same to me!

Now don't you wanna get right with me?
    CHOIR: (Puzzling evidence)
I hope you get ev'rything you need
    CHOIR: (Puzzling evidence)

EVERYONE
    Puzzling evidence
    Puzzling evidence
    Puzzling evidence
    Done hardened in your heart.
    Hardened in your heart.
    ... Alright!

Conspiracies

It's not what you know, it's who you know. Everybody believes in some conspiracy or other. The ones you believe in seem completely plausible. The ones you don't believe in seem like they were thought up by a bunch of nuts and kooks. Can one person be a conspiracy? Was supermarket barcoding prophesied in the Bible?

It is true that a very large percentage of government leaders went to a very small number of prep schools in the East. Sure, they hire each other. Sure, they appoint each other to official posts. So it's true. The world is run by the student council at high school. But those guys didn't go to your high school or mine. It's the high school across town that runs everything. Shakespeare was heavily into conspiracy. Everybody would like to conspire against everybody else ... if we could get away with it, if we could get the chance.

ML

PREACHER Now, listen …

As the song builds, we CUT *occasionally to the screen, which is filled with a succession of* STOCK FILM IMAGES, DIAGRAMS *and* SYMBOLS. *All in support of the vast conspiracy theory … a sample of actual Puzzling Evidence.*

Now I am the gun
And you are the bullet
I got the power and glory!
    CHOIR: (Puzzling)
And the money to buy it!
    CHOIR: (Puzzling)

Got your Gulf and Western and your MasterCard.
    CHOIR: (Puzzling evidence)
Got what you wanted, lost what you had.
    CHOIR: (Puzzling evidence)

EVERYONE
    I'm seeing
    Puzzling evidence
    Puzzling evidence
    Puzzling evidence
    Done hardened in your heart
    It's hardened up your heart.
    … alright!

PREACHER Listen! What I'm saying is *real*.

The song BREAKS DOWN *to a quieter intensity … the drums maintain the rhythm.*

At this point we see Louis edge up toward the Musicians. He whispers something to Ramon … who nods in agreement. Ramon makes a sign to Louis … Louis shakes his head and leaves.

CHOIR
    Huh … huh … huh … huh … huh … huh …
    huh …

PREACHER
    Well, I'm puzzling   CHOIR: Huh!
    I'm puzzling   Huh!
    I'm puzzling   Huh!
    Puzzling   Huh!
    I'm puzzling   Huh!
    Woo … I'm puzzling   Huh!
    Sometimes I'm puzzling! Huh!

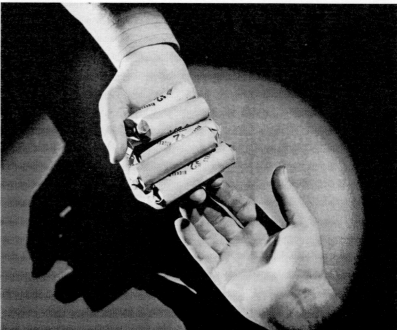

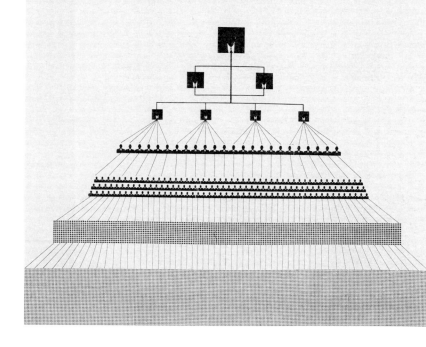

PREACHER   The choice . . . is yours!

PREACHER

See the little children!	CHOIR: Puzzlin'
And the family!	Puzzlin'
Gonna live together!	Puzzlin'
Take them home with me!	Puzzlin'

Well I hope you're happy with what you've made
   CHOIR: (Puzzling evidence)

In the land of the free and the home of the brave
   CHOIR: (Puzzling evidence)

*The Preacher is now heading into the Audience,
continuing to* SING *and* CHANT *all the time.*

The MUSIC *has built up to a frenzy.*

EVERYONE

   I'm seeing
   Puzzling evidence
   Puzzling evidence
   Puzzling (sometimes) evidence
   Done hardened in your heart.
   Hardened in your heart.

MUSIC *continues* FADING *into the background
as we:*

CHOIR

Huh . . . huh . . . huh . . . huh . . . huh . . . huh . . . huh . . .	
I'm puzzling	CHOIR: Huh!
Puzzling	Huh!
Puzzling	Huh!
P-P-P-Puzzlin'!	Huh!
Still Puzzlin'!	Huh!

ML

Exterior, Field on the Flat Landscape—(Day)

*We can see nothing really of interest . . . maybe a
few bushes in the distance, but that's about all . . .
no houses or trees. Suddenly, a* FIGURE, *who must
have been lying on the ground about 30 yards in
front of us, stands up. He has a rifle in his hand. He
slowly looks around.*

HUNTER   I'm hungry . . . You hungry?

*For a minute, we don't know who he's speaking to.
Then another* YOUNG MAN, *also with a gun,
stands up not too far away and looks at his friend.*

Cut to: Exterior, Stage in the Field—(Day)

*Great progress has been made on the stage prepa-
rations for the next day's show. There are now
large sections of the steel framework covered by
corrugated fiberglass, making the structure appear
more like a solid object. Various* WORKERS *are
busy positioning lights and stage gear.*

A MAN *goes up to a microphone at center stage
and begins to test it. We hear a* BOOMING VOICE
over the P.A. *system.*

SOUND MAN   Testing. One . . . Two . . . Hope it doesn't
rain.

The LIGHTS *are being focused on him as he talks
. . . As they* FADE IN AND OUT *he changes colors.*

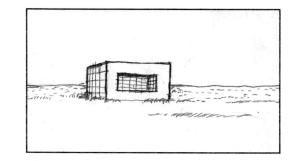

Cut to: Interior, Lazy Woman's Bedroom—(Day)

Close-up of a Video Image

*A detail of a commercial on television. Flashing
lurid colors.* PULL BACK *to* REVEAL . . .

*The television in the bedroom of the Lazy Woman.
She is watching from her bed and flipping through
the channels, using her recently repaired remote
control. She has a plate of food on a tray in front of
her. She* SHOUTS *out comments on the images she
sees to Mr. Tucker, who busies himself repairing
another of her labor-saving devices.*

CP

LAZY WOMAN   Get him! ... Sell it! ... Shake it over here now! ... Tell it! ... Drive over. News at ten. Suits and ties. Hey, Robert, seen this one?

He comes over and has a look, then returns to his work. As she flips from one channel to another (she has a short attention span) we glimpse a new TALKING HEADS VIDEO "LOVE FOR SALE," that incorporates the gestures and style of recent commercials. She continues to flip channels ... round and round. We hear the MUSIC in the background. It seems to continue even through the IMAGES from commercials ... which almost appear to be choreographed to fit the music.

LAZY WOMAN   My favorite shows ... commercials and videos. A toaster flying round the kitchen. Commercial or video?

Mr. Tucker doesn't know. Meanwhile a ROBOT bursts into the room, moves up to the T V and turns and looks.

LAZY WOMAN   Six girls in a brand-new car with the radio on. Commercial or video? A nice steak? ... Or a monster from Washington, D.C.? *Haha!* It's great! They've got that commercial attitude.

CLOSE-UP *of* TALKING HEADS *on television. A spoon automatically goes down and scoops up some of the food on the plate ... She stares ahead as the spoonful of food comes up to mouth level and she takes a bite.*

LAZY WOMAN   They move like sticks. I think they're selling something, but I don't know what it is.

... the VIDEO IMAGES fill the screen. The BAND imitates the movements and attitudes of ads ... Occasionally, real IMAGES FROM ADS are mixed in ... confusing the issue even further. As she says, the Band almost appears to be selling something.

120

SONG: *Love For Sale*

I was born in a house with the television always on
Guess I grew up too fast
And I forgot my name
We're in cities at night and we got time on our
hands.
So leave the driving to us.
And it's the real thing.

And you're rolling
In the blender
With me.
And I can love you
Like a color
TV.

CHORUS

Now love is here
C'mon and try it
I got love for sale
Got love for sale
And now love is here
C'mon and try it
Got love for sale,
Got love for sale.

We see the Lazy Woman in bed reacting to all this.
The ROBOT *is attempting to dance, swiveling*
back and forth.

LAZY WOMAN   Woah, kids! . . . Let me get my devices
in motion.

She inclines her automatic bed and swivels a few
racks and tables.

You can put your lipstick all over my designer
jeans.
I'll be a video for you.
If you turn my dial.
You can cash my check if you go down to the bank
You get two for one
For a limited time.

Push my button . . .
The toast pops up
Love and money
Gettin' all
Mixed up

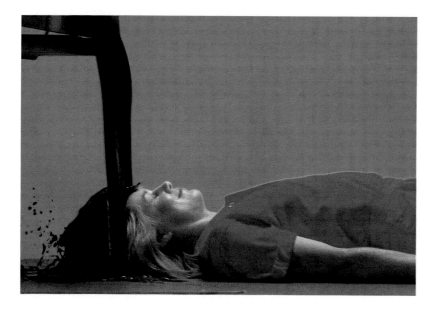

JR

And now love is here
C'mon and try it.
I got love for sale
Got love for sale

Love is here
C'mon and try it
I got love for sale
I got Love
     Love
     Love
     Love
     Love
     Love
     Love
     Love.

LAZY WOMAN *Woah!* ... That's exactly what I was talking about.

The Video/Song is over. The ROBOT *leaves to continue work. On comes an ad Louis Fyne has done for himself. The Lazy Woman is curious.*

LOUIS FYNE *on the television screen:*

LOUIS My name is Louis Fyne and I'm looking for matrimony with a capital M. I believe in the joys and contentment of matrimony. Now, my chances in this world that prints a new diet book every month may not be that good. I'm looking for someone who can accept me for what I am. I'm 6′3″, and maintain a very consistent "Panda Bear" shape.

Louis' telephone number flashes on the screen. 5 4 4 - W. I. F. E.

LOUIS I'm pleased with the way God made me. I wouldn't change a thing. I'm willing to share. (VIDEO IMAGE *of Louis doing a little dance in a field as soothing Muzak plays in the background.*) Please call this number 5 4 4 - W. I. F. E. . . . serious inquiries only.

The Lazy Woman mechanically inclines her bed ... she's fascinated.

LAZY WOMAN Can you believe that ... mmm ... I wonder if he's had much luck.

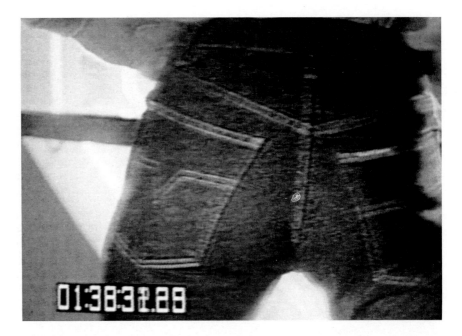

DB

Cut to: Exterior, Housing Development Under Construction—(Day)

We see the flat plain in the background. Some homes have taken shape, while others are merely a framework of two-by-fours. In other spots, there are only markers on the ground, or piles of dirt, to indicate where someone's future home will be.

The NARRATOR *and* CIVIC LEADER *enter the shot.*

CIVIC LEADER (V.O.) I'd like to show you a clear vista of the edge of the civilized world. It's like a game of leapfrog. These houses extend the town further and further out each year. The first family to move in sometimes feels kind of strange . . .

The Narrator and Civic Leader walk around as Civic Leader talks . . . and the CAMERA FOLLOWS.

CIVIC LEADER (V.O.) It's an imaginary landscape. A place to raise your kids. But now not everyone wants kids. Not with the end of the world coming up. Well? . . . would you?

NARRATOR No, not really.

CIVIC LEADER But not before the show tomorrow, huh? *(Laughs; to workers)* Hi, Boys . . . Working hard? . . . Coffee break? You know, it's strange to look at a field and say, "I want the kitchen to be there." Can you imagine? *In the background we can faintly hear what sounds like either* PIGS *or* CHILDREN. Hey . . . do you hear something?

The CAMERA *searches for the source of the* SOUNDS . . . MOVING *between houses and out to the field where a group of* 4-H KIDS *are working with their* ANIMALS.

They point and gesture to them . . . in an attempt to get the beasts to move in some kind of order.

Other KIDS BANG *bits of scrap pipe and lumber together, creating a rhythm that they* SING *to:*

See-through Houses

Houses look best when they're not finished, when you can see through all the different layers and you can tell how they're built. It's great because you can recognize the kitchen and the living room and bedrooms, but you can see right through them and you can see them all at once. When the house is finished you'll never be able to see all that again.

Housing construction, Lucas, Texas

SONG
    I wanna bicycle
    I wanna popsicle
    I wanna space face
    Buy me a cherry face now

CHORUS
    Hey now!
    Hey now!
    Hey now now!
    Hey now!
    Hey now!
    Hey now now!

    I wanna video
    I wanna rock and roll
    Take me to the shopping mall
    Buy me a rubber ball now

    Hey now!
    Hey now!
    Hey now now!
    Hey now!
    Hey now!
    Hey now now!

The kids move closer to us. Each one takes a turn
singing a line, while the others beat a rhythm on
their bits of pipe, wood, and cans.

    Every night sun goes down
    And the people are staying at home
    You can tell your momma & daddy
    leave those children alone

    They know what they're doin'
    They ain't runnin' away
    Uncle John said, "Tell Aunt Mary
    I got nothing to say"
    (And she say:)

REPEAT CHORUS

BRIDGE
    Ho——
    Would the light come hitcha in the eye
    Hey———
    Gonna stop, gonna getcha by surprise!

Every night when the sun goes down
And the people are staying at home
You can tell your momma & daddy
Leave those children alone

They know what they're doin'
They ain't runnin' away
Uncle John said, "Tell Aunt Mary,
I got nothing to say"
(And she said!)

Hey now
Hey now
Hey now now
Hey now
Hey now
Hey now now

Ho————
Would the light come hitcha in the eye
Hey————
Gonna stop, gonna getcha by surprise

*One boy turns and screams out the last verse to no
one in particular.*

I am the king of the world
The boss of the boys & girls
You can live till a 100 & 10
If you listen to what I said

CHORUS
Hey now
Hey now
Hey now now
Hey now
Hey now
Hey now now

Hey now
Hey now
Hey now now
Hey now
Hey now
Hey now now

REPEAT CHORUS
*The kids and their animals disappear into the
housing project.*

130

ML

Cut to: Interior, Middle-Class Home—(Day)

The living room. The walls are filled with hundreds of framed portraits and photographs of relatives. Kay Culver is having a chat over coffee with another WOMAN.

KAY   How far back do you go?

WOMAN   How far back do we go? ... Way back, I would say. *Way* back.

The CAMERA PULLS BACK, *revealing more photos on the walls.*

Kay points at a photo.

KAY   I love the frame on this one ... Is that your second cousin?

The frame is almost identical to all the others.

WOMAN   Oh, now they're something special. A scandal with a duke or something ... It's in some history books, I hear. Died of consumption.

Kay walks around and looks at more photos.

KAY   Oh, I could just stay here all day! This is fascinating.

WOMAN   You know, Mrs. Culver, I think they should teach genealogy in the schools. What do you think? The family ... It's real ... You can touch it ... Forget about that other nonsense.

KAY   I agree.

Cut to: Exterior, Cute Woman's House—(Late Day)

Interior, Cute Woman's Living Room—(Twilight)

Pictures of fluffy kittens, puppies, baby monkeys, and flowers. Chairs with furry covers and planters in the shapes of brightly spotted mushrooms. Everything glows in pastel colors.

The CUTE WOMAN *and* LOUIS FYNE *sit on opposite sides of a carved coffee table, drinking colored sodas.*

Oak Cliff, Dallas

CUTE WOMAN   Do you like animals, Louis?

LOUIS   They're nice when they're small. I had a puppy
once ... got run over though ...

CUTE WOMAN   Aw ... well, what other things do you
like, Louis?

LOUIS   Well, moonlit nights ... pretty music. I'll tell
you the truth, I'm a sucker for romance.

CUTE WOMAN   Oh, you like music? What kind of
music?

LOUIS   I like country music.

CUTE WOMAN   You like country music?

LOUIS   You know I do ... Not that Hollywood country. Hank Williams, Merle Haggard ... Tammy ...
Lefty ... Loretta. Anybody can sing those songs
... if they want to ... and people appreciate that.
Although not everyone can pull it off.

CUTE WOMAN   Music is one of the sweetest things. If
it's sweet, maybe it's cute. There's always room for
more sweetness in the world.

LOUIS   As a matter of fact, I've written a song myself.
Yes ma'am. I'm gonna sing it tomorrow in the
show ... It's about my life. What else do I know,
huh? Give you a little sneak preview here. Hold on
there. I hope you like it. It would mean a lot to
Louis.

Louis stands up and SINGS *a cappella to an imaginary audience. He* HUMS *yet-to-be-written words
in sections. His performance is plain, but obviously from the heart.*

LOUIS

In 1950 when I was born
Poppa mm mmm hm hm
Six foot tall in size 12 shoooes
Mmm hmm da da people like us.

*He turns and stares at the Cute Woman as he
moves into the chorus.*

Duncanville, Texas

134

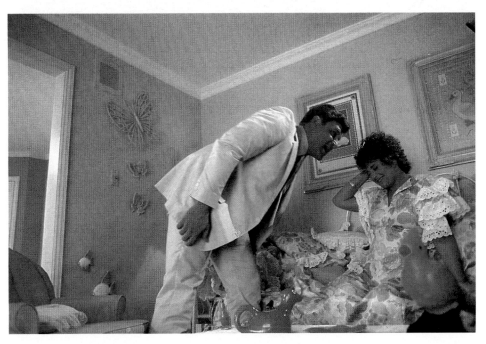

LOUIS

> People like us
> (Who will answer the telephone)
> People like us
> (Growing big as a house)
> People like us
> (Gonna make it because)
> Dum dee mm mm mm
> We just want someone to love.

Louis does a little bow when he finishes.

Ta *daa!* ... what d'you think? Huh?

CUTE WOMAN   Do you know when you sing your eye sockets go way back in your head? It makes your eyes get beady.

LOUIS   But ... Did you like my music?

CUTE WOMAN   It's awfully sad, isn't it? I could never allow such sadness into my life. Do you really feel that way?

LOUIS   I never thought about it. Maybe I am a little sad ... I like sad songs. Make me wanna lie on the floor. *(long pause)* Well, I guess I'll go now ... Sorry. Nice talking to you. Louis the Bear. Out the door.

Louis does another little bow as he gets up and prepares to leave.

CUTE WOMAN   Bye.

Cut to: Exterior, Tex-Mex Club—(Dusk)

Louis's car is there.

Interior, Tex-Mex Club—(Night)

A dance floor in the center, a small stage up front, a bar at the rear and tables around the dance floor with COUPLES *seated listening to the* BAND ... *When the Band plays the men choose partners or stand up with the woman at their table and move onto the dance floor and immediately begin executing the appropriate steps. The dancing is intricate and formalized ... but retains enough looseness not to be stiff.*

La Música Chicana
by Ben Tavera-King

February 1978 Whether it was a song about marijuana laws, brutality by the Texas Rangers or Chicano pride, the issues were covered by Música Chicana. Says Joe Hernández, known as Little Joe: "We still have to look out for ourselves and be proud of our music and the way we live." His audiences respond because they are touched personally. "When I was feeling poor, Little Joe had a song about it," says one fan. "When I came back from Vietnam, he had a song, and, when I became proud of being a Chicano, Little Joe was singing along."

... "Even though it would probably be easier to switch to Top 40 music, we feel like we need to remind the kids about their heritage," says David Márez, lead vocalist of [the] People [Orchestra]. "So we take the music and add our own touches, but we're still *polkeros* in the old sense and our music still has that same old beat."

Accordionists like Esteban Jordan can lay a complicated jazz melody on top of a polka that will rival *salsero* Eddie Palmieri's complex piano flights of fantasy.

Says Tony de la Rosa, a virtuoso accordionist who's played the Música Chicana circuit for the last 20 years: "The whole thing is, when I play the accordion a special way, people can feel it and it touches them somewhere."

The most obvious place it touches them is the feet. Local clubs tucked away in Mexican American barrios find themselves bursting at the acoustic seams on weekends and especially on Sunday afternoons for dances known as *tardeadas.*

Copacabana Club, Dallas

Ramon plays keyboard in the Band, which consists of himself, a DRUMMER, *a* GUITARIST, *a* GUITAR-TYPE BASS, *and* TWO SINGERS, *one of whom plays accordion.*

From across the crowded dance floor we can see Louis ENTER *the Club. He's a little out of place here. As is the usual practice, he is searched for weapons at the door by a stern, short woman. He makes his way across the dance floor in order to talk further with Ramon. He attempts to negotiate the floor passage by dancing in sympathy with the other dancers, riding the undulating rhythms of their bodies to the opposite shore.*

He moves up beside Ramon and makes contact. Ramon talks as he plays.

RAMON   We take a break in 5 minutes ... can you hang?

LOUIS   *(Louis shakes his head)* Did you talk to him?

RAMON   No problem. You got a photograph, right? ... and cash.

Louis nods. Ramon gives Louis a piece of paper with an address written on it, makes a sign signifying everything's cool. Louis heads for the door.

LOUIS   Thanks!

RAMON   Hey ... take it easy!

Ramon smiles at the accordion player as Louis once again attempts to negotiate the dance floor.

Cut to: Exterior, the Poor Part of Town—(Night)

A series of cute little boxy houses. Nice manicured lawns with no trees. One house stands out ... Its yard is chock full of stuff. Car parts painted like faces ... statues covered with Christmas decorations and cast-off clothing ... a hand-lettered sign INVISIBLE HOSPITAL OF ST. JOHN THE BAPTIST.

LJ

We hear faint MUSIC *coming from inside.*

Louis's car drives by slowly and disappears.

Moments later, the same car reappears and parks in front.

Louis Fyne emerges from the car and haltingly heads for the front door. He knocks and the door is answered by a LITTLE BOY *who leads Louis inside.*

Interior, House—(Night)

The boy takes Louis through the living room, where he and his mom were watching TV, to a room partitioned off with beaded curtains. He demands money of Louis, then parts the curtain, allowing him entry. There is an elaborate altar at one end that combines Afro-Atlantic iconography with statues and images of Christian saints. There are icons that are wholly original . . . A sword and a pink telephone . . . A thin aluminum foil trough weaves through the various elements of the shrine . . . Statues of saints dipped in glitter nestled in a cloud of angel hair. There is a pile of twigs and branches on the floor in a corner. A small record player provides music.

The Little Boy introduces Louis to his father and then . . . retreats into the living room.

His father is Mr. Tucker.

LOUIS   Ramon gave me your address. *Louis hands Mr. Tucker a Polaroid of himself.*

MR. TUCKER   Come on in. Come in.

LOUIS   You know, I'm new to this.

MR. TUCKER   *(as he places Louis's Polaroid on the wall among the others there)* It's O.K. You don't have to believe. If you follow directions you can't go wrong. You are wanting to attract love.

LOUIS   How did you know?

MR. TUCKER   Your heart is too large. You are an honest man. I . . .

ML

LOUIS   *Matrimony.* My life. I want to share my life. I've
tried everything . . .

MR. TUCKER   Often our true nature is not what we
might hope it is . . .

Louis looks completely dejected.

MR. TUCKER   In your case you are drawn to love.
Whatever you think is what you get. Love *must* be
drawn to you.

*Mr. Tucker points to a statue wrapped in news-
paper clothing . . . and then to a statue of a Catho-
lic saint.*

MR. TUCKER   This is Ogun and Saint Therese . . . they
are both on your head. I will have to ask them
some questions. Do you dance, Mr. Fyne?

LOUIS   I know a few steps. You mean you can talk to
the spirits about me?

MR. TUCKER   Some of them are Popes . . . They find
me . . . I got lots of Popes passing through my body.
You, sir, are a magnet. You are a man who could
take things easy.

*Louis seems encouraged . . . he's more comfortable
now.*

MR. TUCKER   You see, we all live in a giant magnetic
field. Positive and negative forces are moving
around us.

He puts dried flowers on Louis' chest.

MR. TUCKER   Discharge the negative forces you have
involuntarily received.

*Tucker smacks his hands together, pulverizing the
flowers.*

MR. TUCKER   Remove anything metallic.

Louis takes off his watch and empties his pockets.

MR. TUCKER   This will take some time.

*Louis drops his watch and change into a Zip-loc
baggie that Tucker provides. Tucker hands it back
to him.*

Blackhawk Services,
Israelite Spiritual Church, 1980

Eternal Life Christian Spiritual Church, 1974

Yard Art

Most people's houses are like their
bodies. We're more or less alike on
the outside and yet there's this
incredible tumult and variety of
points of view and opinions going
on inside, most of which we keep
to ourselves. Most houses are the
same way. They look fairly alike on
the outside but people do all this
wild stuff on the inside. They figure
as long as it doesn't get out into the
yard it's all right. Then every once
in a while you see these people that
kind of turn themselves inside out.
They put their inside outside and
maybe they make their placid exterior into their interior. They do
seem to be very calm inside. It's not
for everybody though. Not everybody wants to walk down the street
with his guts hanging out.

The Power

He's got the power. What power?
Well, that depends on what you need.

by John Davidson

[A psychiatric supervisor] at a Houston hospital mentioned that psychiatric patients were occasionally laboring under a voodoo curse . . .

I had learned that folk healers, traditionally shunned if not legally prosecuted in most areas, are now being considered by some physicians as folk psychiatrists more effective in treating culturally predisposed blacks and Chicanos than is the established medical system.

. . . *Curanderos* are religious individuals who have a supernatural gift for healing. They are modest about the gift, never advertise, and accept money only by donation. They make no claims of personal power, as pride, it is thought, would turn the gift against them. Though purveyors of religion and white magic, *curanderos* must know black magic to confound the spells of *brujos* (witches) and are therefore considered potentially dangerous people capable of "working with both hands" . . .

To cure the patient, a *curandera* has him lie beneath a sheet and rubs him with an egg while praying. The egg collects or sweeps up the evil spirits. The ritual is called a *barrida* or sweeping. After the *barrida*, the egg is broken into a dish and placed under the sick person's bed. If an eye forms in the egg, it means the sick person is victim of *mal ojo* or evil eye. The evil is destroyed by burning the egg.

. . . In serious case of *brujería* (witchcraft), a black dove or a black chicken is used to collect the evil and then the bird is sacrificed.

. . . A girl said she knew a woman who had suffered from *susto* (lingering anxiety and debility caused by magical fright). To cure her, the *curandero* spread a handkerchief over her face while she was sleeping, poured whiskey on the handkerchief, and blew. It gave the woman quite a shock, but it cured her . . .

Stanley's is a very special kind of drugstore. In the glass display cases that run along the sides of the shop and across the end, I identified amulets, charms, crucifixes, crystal balls, Vapo-Rub, voodoo dolls, and powders with "alleged" magical powers.

"We lookin' for something to move somebody," a woman told one of the clerks.

"Do you want the Jinx Removing candle or the Send Back candle?" [another] clerk asked [his customer]. "If you want to send the evil back, you'd better use one of these. Burn it an hour each day and read Psalm Twenty-three."

Just as clothes are more fashionable if they come from the right store, voodoo dolls are more powerful if they come from Stanley's . . .

At the 7-African Powers Curio Shop in downtown Houston, a middle-aged man with platinum-blond, razor-cut hair said that their customers weren't just blacks and Chicanos, but included "prominent wealthy people, lawyers, and other professionals."

When I asked the man why people bought voodoo dolls, he said, "Bored. I've noticed everybody's bored since World War II."

. . . At the Invisible Hospital of St. John the Baptist—Spiritual Center of Prayer, Curing, and Culture, I went through the side entrance into a long, empty waiting room and sat down across from two homemade mannequins engaged in struggle. (The white figure in a platinum blond wig was getting the better of the red mannequin.)

A twenty-foot-long altar peopled by a multitude of plaster saints ran along one side of the room and a row of old theater seats painted kelly green lined the other side. At the center of the altar by the kneeling rail, I noticed amid the religious paraphernalia two leather whips, a large curved sword, a red crown of leaping flames studded with eyeballs, and a pink Princess telephone.

The long altar is a vision of the River Jordan that came to Cirilo Sanchez through a dream. He pointed out a thin trough of water that flowed through all the plaster saints that depicted the birth of Christ, the baptism, the Last Supper, and the crucifixion . . .

Tuesday morning I went looking for Mr. Castro, a *curandero* . . . Mr. Castro was happily employed as a school janitor when God gave him the gift of healing. "To tell you the truth," he said, "I didn't want to take it. But then I come to see some lights. I didn't want to see anything, but I started seein' little lights on the floors I cleaned. Little diamonds or sparkles. They was on the little boys' faces too and the color of their faces would change. I was confused. Got so sick I had to leave school. Then they took me to a healer. I wasn't religious, didn't believe in healers, but he said I was one too, so I started going to concentration meetings to be a healer. That was in 1958."

Between 1 p.m. and 1 a.m. six days a week, he sees fifteen or sixteen clients. Most of them come because they have too much on their minds.

To treat patients, Mr. Castro performs a *barrida* with an egg or prescribes taking three parsley baths three days in a row to take away superstitions and drinking three soda waters each day. "Drink half and throw half away."

"I give people orders, but the orders are from God. God tells me."

"Tells you?"

"Yes, I hear God."

"What does he sound like?"

"He sounds like he's from the dead. He has a light voice."

[One Sunday night I attended a concentration meeting, led by Mr. Castro, in West San Antonio.] The impact of the incense-filled dark room was immediate. Above, a large round light pulsed purples and reds like the magnified eye of a fly and there was the echoing sound of a recorded Latin mass. The room was as thick with religious and magical icons as with incense, and it took a moment to sort out the images of Christ, Buddha, and the Virgin Mary among the various saints, spiritualists, and folk saints. Christmas streamers hung from the ceiling and there were three sky-blue pulpits for the sun, the moon, and the stars . . .

Mr. Castro delivered a long invocation to God and the spirits above the sound of recorded religious music and then moved around the circle marking each of us on the throat, the wrists, and forehead with small crosses of scented oil. Music was handed out, we sang . . . Mr. Castro flipped the LPs on the record player.

A refrain from one of the songs on the record player caught my attention: *rompiendo la monotonía del tiempo*: breaking the monotony of time.

LOUIS   I'm going to sing at the show tomorrow. Will this help?

MR. TUCKER   Well, I'll work on you tonight and tomorrow ... In the meantime, do not cross your legs ... That might interfere with the spirits. Take this ...

He presses an amulet into Louis' hands.

MR. TUCKER   Go about your business. Be calm, cool, collected. Drink three soda waters a day. Drink half and throw half away. Think positive. Don't let negative thoughts enter your mind. Have faith—believe—it'll all be right.

Mr. Tucker closes his eyes.

MR. TUCKER   Can you feel it? I am good at everything I do. Your voice is strong. You have nothing to lose but your bad luck.

Tucker spins around ... circling Louis. He then runs his hands down Louis, starting with his head, and working all the way down to his feet. Then he shakes his hands vigorously, as if removing whatever they have accumulated.

MR. TUCKER.   It's over. Go and enjoy your love life. Sayonara.

Tucker returns to the altar, ignoring Louis, who then leaves.

Black out.

We hear the SOUNDS *that the Little Girl made in Scene One in the distance.*

Fade up on: Exterior, Main Street—(Day)

The center of town comprises a four-block area around an intersection. The buildings here are older than the metal prefabs we've seen so much of. There are PEOPLE *lining the sidewalks as the* PARADE *passes by. There are banners across the street. We hear the* SOUND *of* MARCHING DRUMS. *In the background we hear the* VOICE *of an* M.C. *over some speakers.*

Willard Watson, "The Texas Kid"

The Beer Can House, Houston. John and Mary Milkovisch have covered every inch of the outside walls of their house with flattened beer cans.

ML

VOICE OF M.C.   Lookit that flag! The Daughters of the Texas Revolution ... a gift from the Saxon Oil Corp. in Dallas ... a note of thanks ...

We see an OLDER WOMAN *bearing a huge Texas flag parading down the middle of the street. Behind her are a* GROUP *of similar* WOMEN *on decorated bicycles.*

We see a GROUP *of* MARCHING TWIRLERS *in short cowgirl skirts, boots and vests. The Marching Drummers are behind them, and accompany their synchronized routine.*

VOICE OF M.C.   Ladies and gentlemen, the Pleasant Oaks Majorettes ... an experience these gals will never forget. In whatever field they enter, being a Majorette will give them a boost.

A series of quick CLOSE-UPS *of the girls' faces ... they're intense, concentrating ... and overheated. The shots are a series of portraits.*

VOICE OF M.C.   They have to maintain their practice schedule, keep their grades up ... their weight down ... and keep smilin'. Businesses and colleges seek these gals out. Varicorp could use some gals like these ...

We see LOUIS *on the sidelines in a green suit.*

We see another section of the CROWD ... *among them are the* CUTE WOMAN *and the* LYING WOMAN.

VOICE OF M.C.   Yes, it sure is ... you can be sure of that, Bob. *Ho!* It's Grand Marshal Earl Culver and family ... *Thank you Earl!* ... from all of us ... and thanks to Anderson autos for the loan of the car ... a real beauty.

We see the CULVERS *in the parade waving to the Crowd a little and smiling from a huge white convertible. They are all sitting on the top of the back seat ... Earl and Kay on either side, and the*

ML

kids in the middle. Earl says something to his son, who relays it to his mother, who responds to her daughter, who gives the answer to her dad.

On the sidelines, the Lying Woman speaks out to no one in particular.

LYING WOMAN   Such a charming man. Few people know he's got a bull tattooed on his stomach.

The Cute Woman turns to her in amazement.

CUTE WOMAN   Excuse me, honey, Earl Culver? They look so nice! . . . it reminds me of that song "Welcome To My World" . . . Do you know it?

LYING WOMAN   Know it? Honey, I wrote it!

CUTE WOMAN   I'm sorry . . . I must have thought you were someone else.

We see a WHITE FLATBED TRUCK *with paper streamers and a sign announcing the winners of the smiling contest.*

CUTE WOMAN   You know you'd look better if you smiled? Try it, you'll like it! Look! . . .

A group of people are on the back of the truck, some GUYS *and some smiling* LITTLE GIRLS. *They grin at the Crowd.*

We see the GUYS *who were practicing smiling in the factory.*

SMILER #1   This one I call "Tecumseh's last stand."

He smiles.

SMILER #2   We'll see whose last stand it is. Look at this, I call it the "inverted rainbow."

He tries a smile where the corners of his mouth go down instead of up.

VOICE OF M.C.   Take it easy, fellas! . . . *(sings)* . . . the shadow of your smiiiile!

We see the Narrator walk up to Louis at the sidelines. They are wearing almost identical outfits, although Louis' is brighter.

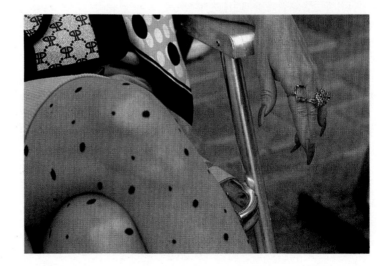

Texas State Fair

Fourth of July Parade, Crowley, Texas

LOUIS Hey!

NARRATOR Hey, the *Bear*.

LOUIS Nice shirt!

NARRATOR Thank you. Nice outfit!

LOUIS Those cheerleaders were good, huh?

NARRATOR Oh, yeah ... and there were lots of them too ... And tiny ... *(to the camera)* I don't know about you, but I find parades rather strange ... They're not always as cheerful as they're supposed to be ... lately, I've seen quite a few really good ones ... and this one is the best ... the folks don't seem to be afraid of their uniqueness ... Maybe that's because they're inventing the town as they go along.

A MONTAGE *of elements from the parade is seen during the preceding speech:*

A group of black motorcycle riders, all wearing fezzes, weave in and out among each other and wave at the crowd.

The Fighting Puma Marching Band marches in formation wearing their brand-new purple-and-white uniforms.

A group of local businessmen and women march down the street carrying their attaché cases.

A sign advertising the local lawn-care center is followed by a group of people pushing lawn mowers in formation.

The 4-H Club kids we saw at the construction site parade their animals.

A family appears to have gotten trapped in the parade by accident. Their station wagon is forced to follow the parade route.

The local football team marches by in uniform.

VOICE OF M.C. If anyone's at home, they're missing a great show here!

Parades

Parades are horrible. People walking down the streets with their tummies hanging out, wearing funny clothes. Bunch of old folks getting heat stroke. Horses dropping their road apples all over, stinking up the street. Most parades are sponsored by the local funeral home. They completely clog up traffic. In most contemporary parades people don't even walk. They just drive down the street showing off how shiny their car is. There's no reason for these things. Nobody makes any money off 'em. Doesn't do anybody any good. The only reason most of the spectators come is because one of their kids is in one of the groups.

Cut to: Interior, Lazy Woman's Bedroom—(Day)

She is watching the parade on television . . . a local news program or similar show. Mr. Tucker has finished work. He waves goodbye, weaves through her devices, and leaves. The Lazy Woman gives the TV a brief glance.

MR. TUCKER   Goodbye, see you Monday.

VOICE OF M.C.   Don't forget the Show tonight sponsored by Varicorp . . . all local talent . . . as good as anywhere's! There'll be chairs, so you don't have to sit on your coolers.

Exterior, Main Street—(Day)

The Cute Woman's attention shifts, she is attracted by something.

CUTE WOMAN   Oh my. Here they come . . . Here they come!

Behind a banner which reads ''THE FUTURE'' we see a procession of BABIES in decorated strollers, row after row of them. They are pushed by their MOTHERS, dressed in pink.

M.C.   Here are your future secretaries, your future Earl and Kay Culvers, your future scientists . . . Why, who knows, one of you might discover the cure for cancer.

The Cute Woman is running up and down the street.

CUTE WOMAN   Oh! . . . Aren't they adorable . . . how dainty! . . . How itsy bitsy! . . . This is my favorite . . . I'm melting.

She runs by the narrator and Louis, who stands silently fingering the amulet he received from Mr. Tucker.

We see CLOSER SHOTS of the Babies. Really fat Babies, Mexican-American Babies, Black Babies, Indian Babies, Babies in costumes . . . Kings and Queens . . . little Cowboys and Cowgirls.

The Cute Woman has broken out into a sweat. This is a dream come true . . . a higher concentration of cuteness would be hard to imagine.

152

CUTE WOMAN   That one's the cutest! … No, no, this one! … But would you look, everybody, at those two over there!

A set of TWINS *in formal attire. The Cute Woman stumbles, and moves rapidly sideways through the* FRAME.

A close-up. She closes her eyes. Squeezes them tight. Her face is flushed. She opens her eyes and runs back for a closer look in case she missed any of the first batch of kids.

She stoops over to talk to some of the Babies.

CUTE WOMAN   Hi there … Do you know what a little doll you are? Ooooh!

She stands up … reels a bit … takes a few steps backward and disappears downward suddenly, out of CAMERA RANGE.

Blackout.

Fade up … the ETHEREAL SOUND *of many accordions … We even see an* ACCORDION MARCHING BAND *behind the group of Babies. They are playing original* MUSIC *that sounds quite unlike what one would expect from accordions. It has a beautiful dreamy quality to it.*

Afterward we see the marching bands, floats, and finally the accordions, all leaving town … continuing to play. FADE OUT.

Fade up on:

Exterior, Outdoor Stage—(Late Afternoon)

The stage, lights and sound are ready. A beautiful red curtain covers the front of the proscenium. A few VOLUNTEERS *are seen in front, setting up rows of folding chairs.*

The CAMERA MOVES *to:*

ML

Exterior, Huge Nearby Parking Lot—(Dusk)

As the light gets dimmer the cars arrive and begin to move around the lot, presumably looking for a prime spot. We hear the SOUND *of their* CAR RADIOS *... snatches of* MUSIC *and* VOICES *which gradually merge into one texture and melody.*

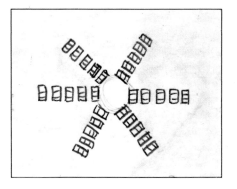

As more cars ENTER, *they all begin to snake around the lot in what is clearly evolving into some kind of synchronized* AUTO BALLET. *What began as a search for parking spaces has turned into a series of stylized movements:*

V formations

Circles ... bumper to bumper.

Groups of cars stop suddenly, to the MUSIC, *and then start again.*

We see the spectacle from directly overhead, revealing the geometric patterns that were not visible from the ground. V's ... S's ... T's ... X's ... O's ... I's ...

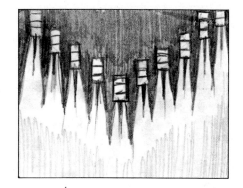

As it gets darker the HEADLIGHTS *from the cars illuminate each other. From above, the beams of light make patterns across the asphalt.*

One by one, the cars come to a stop. Until, within a fairly short period of time, they have all decided on their parking spots. The doors open and the MUSIC STOPS. *We hear a wash of* VOICES *as the people emerge and head into a field.*

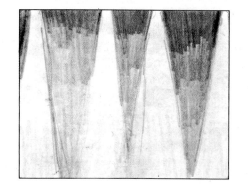

Cut to: Exterior, Stage—(Night)

A podium has been set up in front of the red curtain. A good part of the Audience ... at least those with good seats ... is already seated. EARL CULVER, *the Civic Leader, is talking at the podium.*

CIVIC LEADER   Good evening. We are lucky to be here under the stars. Good to feel good. Feel good about feeling good. Tonight you'll see talent that you can't see on TV (*gestures*) or in the movies (*gestures*). But first I want to tell you a story I

DB

heard in a cafeteria the other day ... God had been working on the Earth round here one day, and when it got dark he had to quit. "In the morning," He said, "I'll come back and make it pretty like the rest of the world, with lakes and streams and mountains and trees."

As the Civic Leader speaks, we see only a CLOSE-UP *of his hands, with which he executes an elaborate series of gestures. Most of these hand gestures have been used throughout the ages by public speakers, but Earl seems to have appropriated an unusually large number of them. He also seems to apply them almost at random; sometimes they seem to connect with or emphasize his patter, and other times they seem to have nothing to do with it whatever. It is almost an abstract dance.*

CIVIC LEADER But when God came back the next morning, He discovered that the land had hardened like concrete overnight! Not wanting to have to start all over again, in His infinite wisdom He had an idea. "I'll make some people who like it this way."

Cut to: CLOSE-UP *of red curtain.*

Exterior, Parking Lot—(Night)

CLOSE-UP *of cars in parking lot.*

Exterior, Stage—(night)

Back to scene:

The curtain begins to part as the Civic Leader announces the First Act.

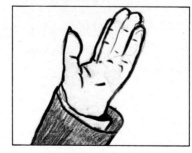

CIVIC LEADER (V.O.) Now I'm going to introduce you to three guys who can tell you more about Texas in five seconds than you'd ever want to know! ... You've seen them on television and at the Fair ... Norman Seaton, Charles Connour, and Randy Erwin ...

ML

MUSIC BEGINS *although there is no band on stage, just* TWO FELLAS *at opposite sides of the downstage end and* ANOTHER GUY *upstage center. They all have microphones. As the* MUSIC BUILDS *and the* SQUARE DANCE RHYTHM *intensifies, the Two Downstage Men, who are professional auctioneers, begin to engage in verbal battle. Each Man* "SINGS" *or* "CHANTS" *as rapidly as possible and is then responded to by the other Man, who tries to outdo him in verbal gymnastics.*

The Audience begins to CLAP *in rhythm, encouraging the competition.*

As the Two Men rap, they slowly edge closer to one another . . . toward downstage center. So does the Third Man, who slowly inches forward from the rear.

At various points, the Man in the rear YODELS *a kind of chorus in response to the duel in front of him.*

The Dueling Auctioneers are now only a few feet from each other . . . chanting directly into each other's faces with a ferocious intensity. Just as they seem about to explode, the Yodeler comes up close, produces a lasso, and, twirling it, ropes all three of them together . . . The auctioneers shake hands, and all break out in wide smiles.

The Audience APPLAUDS *wildly.*

Cut to: Interior, Mr. Tucker's House/Shrine—(Night)

We see Tucker begin to arrange things . . . lighting candles and incense.

Exterior, Stage—(Night)

The Son and Daughter of Earl and Kay Culver are onstage holding ventriloquist's dummies. Other YOUTHS *are off to the side playing miniature handheld synthesizers as background* MUSIC. *The whole group is dressed in frontier outfits.*

LARRY   *(to his dummy)* You tell her that Texas must be free! And no amount of bullying will convince me otherwise.

LARRY'S DUMMY'S VOICE   Living without you is driving me crazy. Woopps! I mean, sign this document and turn Texas over to its rightful owners.

LINDA   *(to her dummy)* You tell him that I never want to see him again ... and that goes for the State Capitol as well ...

LINDA'S DUMMY'S VOICE   Since 1855 I have kept my word. Now you must keep yours ...

The Civic Leader and his wife look on from the wings, enthralled. The rest of the Audience is a little puzzled.

Another YOUNG COUPLE ENTERS ... *this time wearing outfits from a slightly more recent era. They bring out folding chairs, which they place behind the Culver Kids. These new Performers then proceed to manipulate the Culver Son and Daughter as if they were dummies. The* MUSIC *becomes more melodramatic.*

TEENAGE BOY   How often have I told you not to mix with that oil-field trash?

TEENAGE BOY   *(Does Linda's voice as he manipulates Linda)* What I do is between me and Rick.

LINDA'S DUMMY'S VOICE   *(to Teenage Boy)* In the future, these streets will be filled with cars ... may the great State of Texas flourish!

TEENAGE GIRL   President Roosevelt says we are part of a grand plan.

TEENAGE GIRL   *(Does Larry's voice as she manipulates Larry)* You better go home now, Ma. My head's startin' to spin. Politics will kill us all.

LARRY'S DUMMY'S VOICE   *(to Daughter's dummy)* Gimme a kiss, Sugar.

Cut to: Exterior, Stage Wings—(Night)

We see a nervous LOUIS FYNE *mumbling to himself as he watches the unique local acts.*

Texas Monthly

What Texas Means to Me
by Stephen Harrigan

July 1982   When my plane landed in Amarillo the man in the seat next to me nodded toward the window and said, "Pretty, isn't it?"

I'm afraid I gave him a rather blank look, because all I saw through that same window was a vast field of concrete and, far in the distance, the hazy Amarillo skyline, which at first I took to be a cluster of grain elevators ...

Texas is a zone in which the stunning vistas more or less peter out, leaving us with only one great geographical distinction: size. The prudent and prideful Texan takes in the whole package while retaining an affection for the few component parts with the necessary spit and polish to be thought of as scenery. He develops an eye for breadth, along with an ability to look close and hard at the unlovely places and graciously accept them for what they are.

ML

"The Legendary Stardust Cowboy" sings a song and demonstrates some original "hollers."

A MAN twirls sixteen ropes at the same time.

Two MEN stand at opposite sides of the stage and yell insults at each other.

An INVENTOR displays an elaborate device that "works," but doesn't do anything . . . he describes another device that he says is "too secret to show."

A GROUP of CHILDREN wear masks of well-known politicians and world leaders. They engage in a game, in which they fall down . . . squirming in mock agony.

A BAND made up of local teenagers sings a medley of themes from TV shows and commercials.

A COMEDIAN does a series of visual gags using a car body as a prop.

A GROUP of WOMEN twirl briefly across the stage wearing enormous dresses.

Blue Star Line Dancers

Yo-yo champions

True Stories art department

Apache Belles, Tyler, Texas

ML

Cut to: Interior, Mr. Tucker's Altar—(Night)

Mr. Tucker has begun to work on Louis' "cure." We see him finishing attiring himself in white. He looks beautiful. We still hear the SOUND *of the* TELEVISION *which is being watched in the next room, although a* RECORD *of* INSPIRATIONAL MUSIC *that Tucker plays can be heard now as well.*

He lights two candles, and starts his PRAYER:

Divine order, take charge of
my life today and every day
For good, for me, today.
This is a new day for me,
A day I will never see again
I'm divinely guided all day long.
Whatever I do will prosper.

He takes a drink from a bottle shaped like a fish and sprays out the liquid around the altar.

After that he picks up a twig and waves it around, "sweeping" the room.

Divine love, surround me,
Enfold me, and enrapt me.
And I will go forth in peace.
Whenever my attention goes away
From that which is good and constructive,
I immediately bring it back to
The contemplation of that which is
Lovely and of good report.
I am spiritual, mental, magic,
Attracting all things to me that
bless and prosper me.

He puts twig back in the big jar of twigs.

I am going to be a success
In everything I do today.

He points at Louis's Polaroid.

You and me are going to be
happy from now on.

ML

Yaombe! . . . cimbalo! . . . guede nimbo papa!

Tucker then starts to dance and sing, pointing at various candles and totems.

You'll be, hmm-hmm-hmm-hmm, magnet for money
You'll be, mm-mm-mm-mm, magnet for love
You'll feel, hmm, light in your body
Now I'm gonna say, gonna say these words:

He turns to the four directions, his hands up, supplicating. He whispers in Spanish.

Rompiendo la monotonia del tiempo
Rompiendo la monotonia del tiempo

He rubs his hands in a bowl of red dust . . . as if washing them.

It might hmm-mmm-mm-mm . . . it might rain money.
It might hm-hi-hi-hi . . . it might rain fire.
Now I'm gonna call,
Gonna call on Legba.
Get yourself a sign
Get your love and desire.

Turning again . . . crouching, with one hand on his forehead now.

Rompiendo la monotonia del tiempo
Rompiendo la monotonia del tiempo

Suddenly, he leans way back, singing out, loud and clear.

Papa Legba,
Come and open the gate.
Papa Legba,
To the city of camps.
Now, we're your children
Come and ride your horse
In the night
In the night
Come and ride your horse

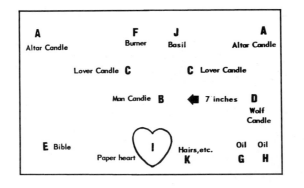

Magical Charms, Potions, and Secrets for Love

by C.A. Nagle

To cause a woman to submit to love . . . Touch the woman and say, "Bestarbeto corrumpit viscera ejus mulieris." This Latin phrase destroys her resistance.

To know if a person is chaste . . . Sap of a radish is squeezed into the hand of the party in question and if there is no fumbling or grappling, purity is indicated.

A love spell . . . The proper mood must be established by advising the woman that you will predict when she will become a bride. Gaining her devout attention and looking her straight in the eye, you will say, "Kafe, Kasita non Kafela et Publia filii Omnibus suis." She will now do whatever you say.

To make a man love you . . . On the altar is placed, as shown in the diagram: A—two white Crucifix altar candles. B—the Man candle. C—two red Love candles. D—the Wolf candle. E—a Bible. F—an incense burner. G—a bottle of Lovers oil. H—a bottle of Compelling oil. I—a piece of parchment paper on which you have drawn a heart. J—a supply of basil leaf. K—something belonging to the man, such as a bit of clothing, no matter how small. Even a thread or two will do. Or some strands of hair. If any of these are impossible to obtain, try to snap a picture of him. A photograph is considered to be of great value in such use. The picture can be taken from near or far.

The Chant
ERZULIE, MATER DOLOROSA
ERZULIE MAPIONNE,
LE BASILIQUE BAPTEME,
CE WANGA OU GANGNIN,
N'A REMECIE ERZULIE.
M'GAIN POUVOI!
M'GAIN POUVOI!
M'GAIN POUVOI!

Do not worry about pronunciation. It is the symbolism and the intent that matters. Say the words as they appear to you.

The Cuban-African Magical System

by Donna Rose

Love . . . A simple spell is to cook a hamburger mixed with the secretions of the body and serve it to the one that is desired.

He makes a circle of red powder on the floor,
surrounding himself.

There is a queen
Of six sevens and nines
Dust in your garden
Poison in your mind
There is a king
That will steal your soul
Don't let him catch you,
Don't let him get control.

Turning faster now ...

Rompiendo la monotonia del tiempo
Rompiendo la monotonia del tiempo

Papa Legba,
Come and open the gate.
Papa Legba,
To the city of camps.
Now, we're your children
Come and ride your horse

He turns once more to the four directions, this
time undulating like a snake.

In the night
In the night, come and ride your horse
In the night,
In the night, come and ride your horse
In the night
In the night, come and ride your horse.

Cut to: Exterior, Stage—(Night)

RAMON *and his* GROUP *are on, performing a full-*
blown version of his song "Radio Head." They all
wear elaborate costumes now and perform in
front of a set. The Band is now augmented by
DANCERS *and various electronic keyboards ...*
although their basic sound is rooted in the Tex-
Mex style.

Ramon executes his dramatic movements, which,
although overly dramatic or completely inap-
propriate for some sections of this song, create a
kind of ironic distance ... as if the song and its
performance exist in separate worlds and times.
It's pretty flamboyant.

ML

Baby your mind is a radio
Got a receiver inside my head
Baby I'm tuned to your wavelength
Lemme tell you what it says:

CHORUS

Transmitter!
Oh! picking up something good
Hey, radio head!
The sound ... of a brand-new world.

So look at my fingers vibrate
From their tip down to my toes
Now I'm receiving your signal
We're gonna leave the land of noise

CHORUS

Transmitter!
Oh! picking up something good
Hey, radio head!
The sound ... of a brand-new world.

The MUSIC BREAKS DOWN *to a jungle beat ...*
Various Members of the Group POUNDING *on*
big drums. Ramon goes into a spinning dance ...
PUNCTUATED *by a strange* ACCORDION IN-
TERLUDE.

As the song resumes, the Audience APPLAUDS.

REPEAT CHORUS

Cut to: Louis in the Stage Wings Watching
Ramon's Act

Louis holds the amulet Tucker gave him ... He
quickly drinks some fluid, then throws half away,
as Mr. Tucker commanded.

Ramon moves around the stage ... back among
the other musicians, jumping up on the drummer's
platform.

Now you and I have no secrets
Now baby, lemme read your mind
I hear ev'rything you're thinking
You can't help the way you sound

CHORUS

    Transmitter!
    Picking up something good.
    Hey! radio head!
    The sound ... of a brand-new world

    Oh! Radio head
    Radio head
    Radio head
    Radio head

    APPLAUSE *from part of the audience. The rest are
a little puzzled.*

Cut to: Exterior, Stage—(Night)

LOUIS *is walking onstage with new-found confidence and energy. The Band is* PLAYING *the opening chords to his song, "People Like Us." He is a new man ... he even seems bigger than before, although that is impossible. When he reaches center stage, he looks at the Audience, then turns around to the Band and, winking, he does a mock* BEAR ROAR. *He turns back to the mike and begins to* SING, *full of confidence. It's a Country and Western song, just like the ones that Louis loves.*

    In 1950 when I was born
    Papa couldn't afford to buy us much
    He said be proud of what you are
    There's something special 'bout people like us

CHORUS

    People like us
    (Who will answer the telephone)
    People like us
    (Growing as big as a house)
    People like us
    (Gonna make it because)

    We don't want freedom
    We don't want justice
    We just want someone to love.
    Someone to love.

    I was called upon in the 3rd grade class
    I gave my answer and it caused a fuss
    I'm not the same as ev'ryone else
    And times were hard for people like us

REPEAT CHORUS

Cut to: Interior, the Lazy Woman's Bedroom—

She's watching Louis' performance on her television. She is obviously impressed . . . She mechanically inclines the bed for a better look.

LAZY WOMAN Is this the same guy who made that commercial for himself?

Louis' song continues in background.

She GETS OUT OF BED *and makes her way over to a telephone and begins to dial.*

Back to: Exterior, Stage—

Louis is at the edge of the stage, singing to the audience.

LOUIS

What good is freedom?
God laughs at people like us
I see it coming
Like coming down from above

The clouds roll by and the moon comes up
How long must we live in the heat of the sun?
Millions of people are waitin' on love
And this is a song about people like us

CHORUS

People like us
(Who answer the telephone)
People like us
(Growing big as a house)
People like us
(Gonna make it because)
We don't want freedom
We don't want justice
We just want someone to love.

Someone to love.
Someone to love.
Someone to love.

Quick cut: The Audience APPLAUDING, *obviously touched.*

Cut to: Interior, Stage Wings—

Louis comes off stage. He is handed a phone.

Cut to: Houses lit by the moonlight. We faintly hear the SOUNDS *of the Little Girl from Scene One.*

Time Lapse—(Day)

The stage is being dismantled . . . slowly returning to a field.

Exterior, the Lazy Woman's House—(Morning) Lots of cars parked outside.

Interior, Lazy Woman's Bedroom

LOUIS FYNE *and the* LAZY WOMAN *are both in bed together. Fully dressed. They* GIGGLE *at each other. There are lots of other people in the room . . . crowding around, taking snapshots and drinking champagne out of plastic cups. A* PRIEST *shakes hands with well-wishers. Louis looks away . . . He stares out the window . . . He isn't really looking at anything, just trancing out. The* SOUND *disappears . . . all we hear is Louis'* VOICE.

LOUIS (V.O.) We are not worrying
We are watching it and doing it
at the same time.
And the family *is* the center of the world.
We are doing what we want to.
Think of the possibilities.
Part Two.
This is Part Two.
I am singing in my sleep.
Is everybody ready?
OK?
Let's go.

One of Louis' Co-workers from Varicorp breaks Louis' reverie when he YELLS *out. The* SOUND *of the celebration returns.*

WORKER The life of Riley! I tell ya! Where are you going on your honeymoon? Louis?

LAZY WOMAN The Bear is staying with me. *(to Louis)* Have you seen Robert?

ML

Cut to: Exterior, a Graveyard—(Day)

A tiny plot surrounded by the vast endless plains. The Narrator and Mr. Tucker stand side by side and watch as someone is buried. There are a few MOURNERS *around . . . some* CHILDREN *with picnic baskets too. The casket is covered with flower decals and cute little stickers, exactly like those the Cute Woman likes. A couple of her lawn ornaments are placed by the grave site. The Lying Woman stands on tiptoe and looks down into the grave as the casket is lowered.*

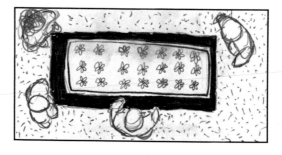

LYING WOMAN   She was my best friend . . . We had so much in common.

Mr. Tucker talks quietly to the Narrator.

MR. TUCKER   She'll come back . . . It'll all come back. My, my.

He looks around at the landscape as he walks away from the grave site. The narrator follows.

This was once all underwater. It's true. I dig sometimes . . . found some sharks' teeth . . . fish bones. Keep them in a jar. Scientists are just discovering this now.

The other Mourners begin to disperse as well, all moving off in different directions as if scattered by the wind . . . Moving out across the plain into the distance. Mr. Tucker and the Narrator turn toward the road and continue to talk.

MR. TUCKER   Respect . . . *Everything* demands respect . . . We must do everything in the right order . . . It's possible to remember every living thing. I can. I write it all down . . . It must be done. Or things will fall apart. You know what I'm talking about?

NARRATOR   I believe I do . . . But I'm not sure. See, I like forgetting . . .

When I see a place for the first time . . . I notice everything, the color of the paper, the sky, the way people walk, doorknobs, every detail.

ML

Then, after I've been there for a while, I don't notice them anymore. Only by forgetting can I remember what a place is really like ... so maybe for me forgetting and remembering are the same thing.

We hear, very faintly, the SOUNDS *of the Little Girl from Scene One once more.*

Huh?

Hey, do you hear something?

The Narrator turns his head to look for the source of the sounds.

Cut to: The Little Girl on the road

The same from Scene One ... Making her SOUNDS. *The shot is practically identical to the first one we saw, except that now she is walking away from us until she disappears.*

She occasionally executes one of her unique and charming gestures along with her sounds.

The LITTLE GIRL'S SOUNDS CROSS FADE INTO THE CLOSING SONG.

ALL CREDITS.

Venus, Texas

DB

"CITY OF DREAMS"

  Here where you are standing
  The dinosaurs did a dance
  The Indians told a story
  Now it has come to pass

  The Indians had a legend
  The Spaniards lived for gold
  The white man came and killed them
  But they haven't really gone

CHORUS
  We live in the city of dreams
  We drive on the highway of fire
  Should we awake
  And find it gone
  Remember this, our favorite town

  From Germany and Europe
  And Southern U.S.A.
  They made this little town here
  That we live in to this day

  The children of the white man
  Saw Indians on TV
  And heard about the legend
  How their city was a dream

CHORUS
  We live in the city of dreams
  We drive on the highway of fire
  Should we awake
  And find it gone
  Remember this, our favorite town

  The Civil War is over
  And World War One and Two
  If we can live together
  The dream it might come true

  Underneath the concrete
  The dream is still alive
  A hundred million lifetimes
  A world that never dies

CHORUS
  We live in the city of dreams
  We drive on the highway of fire
  Should we awake
  And find it gone
  Remember this, our favorite town

   End

Suburban development, Alvaredo, Texas

LJ

Grateful acknowledgment is made for permission to reprint excerpts from the following copyrighted material:

In Advance of the Landing: Folk Concepts of Outer Space by Douglas Curran. Published 1985 by Abbeville Press. Reprinted by permission of the Publisher.

"Why Do Hot Dogs Come in Packs of 10 and Buns in 8s and 12s?" by John Koten in *The Wall Street Journal.* Reprinted by permission of The Wall Street Journal. Copyright © 1984, Dow Jones & Company, Inc. All rights reserved.

Magical Charms, Potions and Secrets for Love by C. A. Nagle. Copyright © 1972, Marlar Publishing Co., Box 17038, Minneapolis, MN 55417.

"Suburban Malls: the Stages for Pantomime Music" by Clifford D. May; and "Cathedrals of Consumption" by Grady Clay in *The New York Times Company.* Copyright © 1985, The New York Times Company. Reprinted by permission.

"The Night of the Hackers" by Richard Sandza in *Newsweek.* Copyright © 1984, Newsweek, Inc. All rights reserved. Reprinted by permission.

"Remote Control Panels That Do It All" by Joseph Giovannini; "Suburban Malls: the Stages for Pantomime Music" by Clifford D. May; "The Great Oil Era Ends in Texas" by Robert Reinhold and "Cathedrals of Consumption" by Grady Clay in *The New York Times.* Copyright © 1984, 1985, The New York Times Company. Reprinted by permission.

"The Night of the Hackers" by Richard Sandza in *Newsweek.* Copyright © 1984, Newsweek, Inc. All Righs Reserved. Reprinted by permission.

"The Bang Behind the Bucks the Life Behind the Style" and "Bummed to the Minimum, Hacked to the Max" from *Newsweek/ Access* published by Newsweek, Inc. Copyright © 1984, Newsweek, Inc. All rights reserved. Reprinted with permission.

Article on "Stereo Coats" in "Everything Under the Sun," "Shoes That Protect Valuables," and "The Way You Walk and Dress Can Make Your Legs Look Great" in *Sun.* Reprinted by permission of Sun, Globe Communications Corp.

"Broke in the Promised Land" by Peter Applebome in *Texas Monthly,* issue of July 1982; "Behind the Lines" by Gregory Curtis, April 1984 and June 1984; "The Power" by John Davidson, June 1977; "Wal-Marts Across Texas" by Rod Davis, October 1983; "Post-Modern Times" by Michael Ennis, November 1985; "What Texas Means to Me" by Stephen Harrigan, July 1982; "Birth of a New Frontier" by Harry Hurt III, April 1984; "A Call to Farms" by Nicholas Lemann, December 1978; and "Death of a Computer" by Joseph Nocera, April 1984. Reprinted with permission of Texas Monthly. Copyright © 1977, 1978, 1982, 1983, 1984, 1985 by Texas Monthly.

Time-Life Library of America/The South Central States by Lawrence Goodwyn and the Editors of Time-Life Books. Copyright © 1967, Time-Life Books Inc.

"Lonely Bachelor Hungers for Love," "Date with Disaster," "World's Laziest Lady," "Loving Couple Hasn't Spoken in 31 Years," and "Your Pants Can Kill You" in *Weekly World News.* Courtesy of Weekly World News.

Author's Note

Although the name of the movie is *True Stories,* I am saddened and disappointed to have to admit that a lot of the stories are made up. Although I was indeed inspired by newspaper articles, and books and magazine articles that are purported to be about real people, I used the stories mainly as inspiration. It seems to give the movie an extra little bit of excitement to think that maybe it could be true. You know, we made up names for the characters inspired by the real people in the articles; some of the characters are combinations of real people; and the real people certainly didn't all live in the same town. You know, I'm not even sure the magazine articles are accurate. To tell you the truth, I don't even really care. What's important is that I believed they were true when I read them. And what's important in this book and in the film is that the spirit rings true. I hope that the people in these articles are real because they certainly did inspire me.

PHOTO AND DRAWING CREDITS

ABOUT THE AUTHOR

Lead singer, songwriter, and guitarist of the rock band the Talking Heads, David Byrne has recorded ten albums with the Talking Heads and has produced and directed seven music videos, several of which are in the Museum of Modern Art's permanent collection.

Stop Making Sense, the feature-length Talking Heads concert film conceived by Byrne and directed by Jonathan Demme, was awarded "Best Documentary of 1984" by the National Society of Film Critics. In 1985, Byrne received MTV's "Video Vanguard" award for his innovative work in music video. *Little Creatures,* the Talking Heads' most recent album, was named "Best album of 1985" by the *Village Voice* and *Rolling Stone* critics polls.

Trained as a visual artist at the Rhode Island School of Design, Byrne collaborated with choreographer Twyla Tharp on her Broadway production of *The Catherine Wheel,* for which he composed and performed an original score. In 1984 he collaborated with avant-garde playwright Robert Wilson, writing the music and text for the "The Knee Plays," short vignettes between the scenes of Wilson's epic opera *The CIVIL WarS.*

Responding to the gap between the rock-music-video form and Broadway musicals, in early 1984 Byrne began to write the original screenplay for *True Stories,* creating a new musical/theatrical form. The film was shot in Texas and edited in Los Angeles.

Born in Scotland in 1952, Byrne moved to Baltimore when he was seven years old. He now lives in New York and Los Angeles.